"Are you afraid I'll take advantage of you when we're out in the wilderness alone, that I'll be overcome by lust?" Sid asked angrily.

Before Alyson could answer, he reached out, fingering the stray curls on her cheek, then moved his hand to cup her smooth neck. "It's definitely something to think about," he whispered roughly.

She couldn't move. Something strange was happening to her. It couldn't have anything to do with the warm hand on her neck. It must be fear, that was it. She was paralyzed with fear, she decided, as a shiver of something that was definitely not fear shook her.

"Yeah," he said. The word was a touch of warmth on her cheek. "It might be nice to see what your type of woman feels like. I've always wondered. Does passion rip through you? And if it does, do you demand to be loved, or do you remember to say 'please' and 'thank you?' Does your body get all hot when you make love"—he moved one hand across her shoulder—"or does it stay cool? Are these lips ever swollen with kisses, or do you keep them firmly pursed?" He brushed his lips lightly across hers. "Yeah, it just might be worth finding out. . . ."

WHAT ARE *LOVESWEPT* ROMANCES?

They are stories of true romance and touching emotion. We believe those two very important ingredients are constants in our highly sensual and very believable stories in the *LOVESWEPT* line. Our goal is to give you, the reader, stories of consistently high quality that may sometimes make you laugh, sometimes make you cry, but are always fresh and creative and contain many delightful surprises within their pages.

Most romance fans read an enormous number of books. Those they truly love, they keep. Others may be traded with friends and soon forgotten. We hope that each *LOVESWEPT* romance will be a treasure—a "keeper." We will always try to publish

LOVE STORIES YOU'LL NEVER FORGET
BY AUTHORS YOU'LL ALWAYS REMEMBER

The Editors

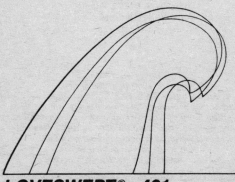

LOVESWEPT® • 431

Billie Green
Sweet and Wilde

BANTAM BOOKS
NEW YORK • TORONTO • LONDON • SYDNEY • AUCKLAND

SWEET AND WILDE

A Bantam Book / October 1990

LOVESWEPT® *and the wave device are registered
trademarks of Bantam Books, a division of
Bantam Doubleday Dell Publishing Group, Inc.
Registered in U.S. Patent
and Trademark Office and elsewhere.*

*If you would be interested in receiving protective vinyl
covers for your Loveswept books, please write to this
address for information:*

> Loveswept
> Bantam Books
> P. O. Box 985
> Hicksville, NY 11802

ISBN 0-553-44062-4

Published simultaneously in the United States and Canada

---

*Bantam Books are published by Bantam Books, a division
of Bantam Doubleday Dell Publishing Group, Inc. Its trademark, consisting of the words "Bantam Books" and the
portrayal of a rooster, is Registered in U.S. Patent and
Trademark Office and in other countries. Marca Regis-
trada. Bantam Books, 666 Fifth Avenue, New York, New
York 10103.*

PRINTED IN THE UNITED STATES OF AMERICA

OPM   0 9 8 7 6 5 4 3 2 1

To Jeanie and James for showing me how fresh and new a seasoned love can be.

Prologue

The Past: *Texas, Somewhere West of the Pecos River*

Paco was a small, wiry man, able to climb the crumbling rock face easily. The perspiration drenching his shirt was not from heat or exertion but from excitement. And from fear. Although he had taken care to leave no trail behind him, at times he felt a crawling sensation on the back of his neck. As though he were being observed. As though he were not alone.

Maybe the god the villagers worshiped so fervently knew what he had done and was watching now, Paco thought with a silent, mocking laugh.

Minutes later, he pulled himself up to the next level, fifty feet below the top of the mesa. He had made it. No one could stop him now.

After pushing aside a pile of brush, he moved forward and disappeared into a narrow crack in the rock. He was ten feet into the natural corridor before the lowered temperature began to chill the perspiration on his body. Shuddering violently, he pressed on, more deeply into the rock. When he was several hundred feet into the imperceptibly rising passage, it abruptly widened.

Darkness obscured his vision, but Paco held the interior terrain fresh in his memory. Before him was a deep, upward-sloping cavern. Dropping to his hands and knees, he searched the rock floor until he found the torch he had left there two days earlier. But even with the light from the torch, he managed to trip over fallen rock several times on his way to the upper end. Long minutes passed before he finally reached the back of the cave. Moving his hands over the wall of stone, he found the niche. The eye-level recess, carved into solid rock by ancient water—or ancient people—was not more than a foot wide and perhaps two feet high. After clearing the small area of dust and rock particles, Paco paused for a moment and leaned against the rock wall to catch his breath, then reached inside his shirt to withdraw his burden. He ran shaking fingers over the smooth contours of the object before carefully placing it in the center of the miniature alcove.

It was done. As soon as the furor died down, as soon as the villagers gave up their frantic but futile search and returned to their sickly little farms, Paco would come back to retrieve his treasure, the treasure that guaranteed his future with the lovely Bonita.

Inhaling deeply, he returned to the entrance of the cave, extinguishing the torch before he entered the narrow passage. Now, when he no longer felt the urgency of his task, when he no longer felt the cold weight of his treasure against his belly, the corridor seemed longer and blacker. Time, solitude, and the enveloping darkness began to work on him. Again he felt eyes upon him. Eyes that could see through the darkness. Eyes that could see into a man's soul. Paco had defied the law. He had defied the god himself.

The superstitious villagers had affected him, he told himself. If the god existed, he wasn't interested in the fortunes of one poor Mexican village.

It was only seconds later that Paco heard the snake. The sound was unmistakable and brought an immediate unthinking reaction. Whipping out his revolver, he shot three times—wildly, blindly—aiming in the general direction of the terrible dry rattle. The flashes of light were followed instantly by the sound of bullets ricocheting off the rock, echoing eerily through the cave.

Then from directly above him came a sound, a sound that pulled Paco's heart into his throat.

His last thought as tons of rock fell upon him was that maybe the villager's god was interested after all.

On top of the mesa the earth trembled. Two hundred feet from the northern edge, a small depression began to form. Hours later, as the soil and fine rock slid downward, an opening appeared. Even later, when the dust had settled and moonlight began to filter through the rupture, a slender golden figure, resting serenely in its stone alcove, was softly illuminated.

One

The Present: *Texas, Somewhere West of Downtown Dallas*

"This is your old hangout?" Alyson Wilde glanced at the thirteen-year-old boy walking beside her. "This is the Shangri-La for which you pine?"

Lenny Doyle drew in a breath of the sour air. "Baddest place in town," he said with satisfaction.

"Bad," she muttered. "I don't know whether I should be correcting your grammar or your taste." She glanced around at the drab buildings lining the street. Weeds grew up through the cracks in the sidewalk, and from the alleys came mysterious pungent odors. "I don't know exactly what it is, Lenny, but somehow I don't seem to fit in."

"It's your clothes. I told you not to dress up."

"What's wrong with the way I'm dressed?" She touched her dusty blue linen slacks. "You said casual. This is as casual as I get."

"You've got scarves and earrings and stuff," he

complained. "You should be wearing jeans and sneakers."

"I refuse to be mugged in my gardening clothes."

When he laughed, Alyson couldn't help smiling. She loved hearing Lenny laugh. Most of the time he was moody and distant, and it was difficult to remember he was just a boy. A small boy. It was only his mouth and personality that were big. Behind the smart mouth, behind the false bravado, was a little boy who had been hurt more than any child should be hurt.

In her preoccupation Alyson bumped into someone traveling in the opposite direction on the sidewalk. It was a woman of indeterminate age. A dark blue golf cap almost covered her wiry steel-gray hair, and she wore a faded pink sundress over a bright orange sweater.

"I'm sor—" Alyson began.

"Stick it in your ear," the woman muttered without bothering to look up.

"Yes, ma'am," Alyson said meekly to the woman's departing back.

"Hey, Sheba!" Lenny called, then to Alyson, "That's Sheba."

"A friend of yours?" she asked dryly.

The older woman kept walking, ignoring Lenny's greeting. "She must be Antoinette today," he said. "Sid says Sheba's got half a dozen people living in her, but only two of 'em are worth knowing."

"Sid says, Sid says," Alyson mimicked silently. For the last two months she had heard in too much detail what the ubiquitous Sid Sweet said.

Mr. Sweet had something to say about everything, and what he said was usually crude. Although Alyson had never met Lenny's friend, she had formed a crystal-clear mental picture of him—bright print shirt open to the waist; long hair slicked back on his head; gold chains, three at least, decorating his thick neck and hairy chest; rings on several fingers, including a gold-nugget pinky ring; and, inevitably, a toothpick clamped between his teeth.

Lenny pointed to a pawnshop in the middle of the block. "That's his place. You sure you don't want to come in and meet him? He's real interesting."

"No," she said without a bit of hesitation. "I think I've met my quota of interesting people today. I'll go catch a movie. That will give you a couple of hours to catch up on things with Mr. Sweet; then I want you to meet me at the drugstore. Two hours, understand?" She frowned as she surveyed the street. "I know this is your territory, Lenny, but just to please me, will you not go anywhere else? See your friend, then go straight to the drugstore. Okay?"

"Whatever," he mumbled, moving away from her. "Catch you later."

Alyson watched until he entered the shop, then turned away with a sigh. For a few minutes today she had thought Lenny was finally beginning to like her, but now she knew his good mood was only due to his being back in his old neighborhood, back where he had once lived with his mother.

Lenny was Alyson's second cousin, her cousin

Blair's son. *Blair.* Just thinking of him brought an aching tightness to her throat. Blair had been her hero. When his parents died in a boating accident, Blair had come to live with Alyson and her parents. She liked him immediately. Blair didn't despise her for being six years younger and sickly. He treated her with loving affection. Soon he was her best friend. Later he had become her idol. Her hero. Even as a teenager, he had been an exceptional artist, but most important, he was the most caring man Alyson had ever known.

Then one day Blair was gone. Alyson had always suspected there had been harsh words between Blair and her father, but she had never had the nerve to ask. She knew only that her cousin had cut them off completely. He hadn't invited them to his wedding, and they weren't informed until several years later of the birth of his son.

It had been a little over six years ago when they received a short letter from Sandra, Blair's wife, informing them of her husband's death in a little town near the Mexican border, and suddenly it was too late. Too late to see Blair. Too late to say one last good-bye at his funeral. It was even too late to meet Blair's son because his widow had already taken Lenny and moved on.

Then, six months ago, Sandra had turned up in Dallas. She said she wanted Lenny to get to know his father's family. Because her parents were now living in Canada, Alyson represented the family, and she tried to get to know the boy. She had desperately wanted to see Blair in Lenny, but it was impossible. Lenny was Lenny, a child on the outside but on the inside—old. Old and cynical.

After several months of using Alyson as a part-time babysitter, Sandra had dropped by one day to announce that she had been offered an excellent job in Los Angeles. Alyson wouldn't mind keeping Lenny for a few days, would she? Just long enough for Sandra to find a decent apartment and get settled in. Just long enough for her to find a place good enough for Lenny.

Although Alyson had resented being used by Sandra, she agreed to let the boy stay with her. As difficult as he was, Lenny was Blair's son. And beneath the turbulent surface was a boy Alyson badly wanted to love if Lenny would give her a chance. So she moved him into one of her guest bedrooms and slowly, painfully began to establish a relationship with her young cousin.

When a week passed without a word from Sandra, Alyson began to worry. After two weeks Alyson was not only worried but extremely annoyed. Eventually she had to consider the possibility that something had happened to Sandra. Strangely, Lenny didn't seem to notice that his mother hadn't been in touch with him. He never spoke of Sandra, and he asked no questions.

One day, three and a half weeks after Lenny had come to stay with her, Alyson picked up the telephone and dialed information, asking for the telephone number of the Los Angeles Police Department. But before she could dial the number, Lenny spoke, directly behind her.

"You don't have to call. The whole thing was a scam. Judas priest, you're dumb. Don't you know she dumped me? On you. She dumped me right on you! There wasn't any job. She's not even in L.A. She went off with some man she met."

Alyson studied his tight angry features for a moment. "Do you know where she is?" she asked quietly.

He shook his head. "She said I wouldn't need to know because you would be my family now." He laughed, and it was the most painful sound Alyson had ever heard. "Are you gonna call the social workers?"

The hurt and anger she could understand, but there was something else in his eyes. Resignation. Deadly, dull resignation. And it broke Alyson's heart.

"Your mother was right," she said, keeping her voice calm and matter-of-fact. "I am your family. And if you're going to be here permanently, we should do something about redecorating your room. You can choose something more appropriate for a . . . young man."

He stared at her silently then swung away, but not before she had seen the sheen of tears in his eyes. That was when Alyson had begun to hate Sandra.

The next two months hadn't been easy. Lenny continued to keep his feelings under a tight rein, and every time they seemed to get closer, he would pull away.

We'll make it, she told herself as she walked down the unfamiliar street. They had to make it. It was their only option. That was one of the reasons they were in this part of town today. Alyson wanted Lenny to know that she wasn't going to try to change him. She wanted him to know that she would allow him to be himself.

But was she being honest? she wondered, frowning slightly. Didn't she want him to change, just a little? She did want him to forget the weeks he had spent in this part of town. She wanted him to forget how often his mother had left him on his own to wander the streets. Lenny had told her enough about his past for her to know that Sandra rarely knew or cared where her son was. And because of the careless freedom his mother had allowed him, Lenny had made some highly questionable connections. Connections like Sid Sweet.

Alyson had come to the point of flinching at the sound of the man's name. While she knocked herself out trying to break through Lenny's defenses, Sid Sweet had done it instantly. Carelessly, without even trying. And Alyson had heard enough about the man to know he wasn't the right role model for a thirteen-year-old boy. When she thought of some of the pearls of wisdom he had passed on to Lenny, she didn't know whether to laugh or grind her teeth.

A couple of weeks earlier she had been trying to explain to Lenny why, at the ancient age of twenty-six, she had never married, and inevitably she heard the two words she had come to dread: *Sid says.*

"Somehow I don't think the insight of Sid the Bookie is what we need right now," she said, fighting to keep jealousy out of her voice.

"He's not a bookie. He's a bail-bondsman and pawnbroker."

"I stand corrected. That certainly qualifies him to be a spiritual guide." She sighed in resignation. "Go on, tell me what Sid says."

"He says relationships are like handkerchiefs. Everybody used to carry a nice cotton handkerchief. They were strong and durable. If you took care of your handkerchief, it would last you forever. But these days people use Kleenex. You ever tried to blow your nose on a Kleenex more than a couple of times? It won't work. They fall apart. You can't take care of a Kleenex 'cause they're not for the long haul." He grinned. "But Sid says they're real handy to have around when you feel a sneeze coming on."

Alyson held off an explosion by biting her bottom lip and counting to ten. *He's not comparing women to Kleenex*, she told herself in an attempt at objectivity. The man was probably referring to the transient quality of modern relationships.

Being objective didn't help. She still wanted to stuff a couple of Sid Sweet's disposable relationships down his cynical throat.

"I don't think your Mr. Sweet is an expert on personal matters," she said carefully. "He's giving you the wrong idea about—"

"Sex?"

"About relationships," she amended.

"I'm thirteen. I need to know about stuff like that."

Alyson had spent the next hour explaining about men and women, and the various ways they interacted. Although Lenny had listened to her, she knew Sid Sweet's words held more weight with the boy. He was the strong masculine image Lenny had been missing since his father's death.

But he's wrong, Alyson told herself. *Damn him, Sid Sweet is the wrong hero for Lenny.*

Sid sat in his small office, hunched over a stack of papers, swearing at them as though they were living, deceiving beings. He hated doing the books.

This is the price of success everybody's always talking about, he told himself with a grimace of discontent. For success, he'd had to give up the things that brought him into the business in the first place. Sid liked working with people. He got a kick out of talking to them and swapping stories with them. But in the last two years he had bought two more pawnshops and had to turn over the part he loved to managers. Which was why he was now sitting in a stuffy little office, swearing at a bunch of stupid numbers.

"If you don't do your homework, you'll fail math. You've got a bad attitude, Sid, and unless you straighten out, you'll never to amount to anything."

Sid couldn't recall the teacher's name, but he could still see her face. If he tried, he could see a long line of disapproving faces, culminating with a small woman with porcelain skin, Mrs. Bartlett, his grandfather's employer.

"Stay away from my daughter or I will be forced to find another gardener. I respect your grandfather, and I would hate to lose him, but

Audrey is an innocent. She isn't capable of dealing with someone like you."

The precious Audrey had faded from his memory, but he would never forget Mrs. Bartlett. Her words she had spoken as she gazed at a spot somewhere over his shoulder were burned into his brain. Over the years there had been other words, thrown at him with varying degrees of contempt and anger by a number of different people, but the meaning was always the same: *You're worthless, Sid.*

Suddenly the accounts on the desk in front of him didn't seem so bad. Sid had fooled them all. He was worth something. In fact he was worth quite a lot.

When he heard a knock on his office door, satisfaction in his success didn't keep him from being grateful for the interruption.

"Yeah?" he yelled.

Sid leaned back and smiled at the thin blond boy who walked in. Sid liked Lenny Doyle. Lenny was never going to be conventionally attractive—his features were too large for his face, and his limbs too long for his body—but there was something about him that one noticed. Lenny was not easily forgotten. He was a survivor, as Sid had been at that age.

"Lenny, my man," Sid said. "I haven't seen you in a coon's age. I thought maybe you ran off with that tattooed lady we saw at the carnival."

The boy laughed, and after petting the dog sleeping in the corner of the room, he slumped down in the chair facing Sid's desk.

"So what are you doing in my part of town?"

Sid asked. "You get paroled from that fancy prison you've been living in, or did you bust out? Does Miss Manners know you're here?"

Lenny shifted uncomfortably. "She brought me. You know, she's not so bad really. She doesn't yell when I get my clothes dirty or nothing."

Sid hid a frown. He was going to have to watch what he said about Lenny's new guardian. He shouldn't push his prejudices on the kid. Lenny had enough to deal with, the poor little bastard. His mother had been a world-class witch, but Sid had a feeling Miss Manners was going to be even worse. He knew her type well—prissy-proper without one ounce of compassion in her overindulged body, the kind who liked to tell other people they weren't worthy of living in the same world. He wanted to warn Lenny not to get too close to her, because when she had had enough of playing Good Samaritan, she would dump the kid, just as his mother had done. And even if she let him stay, it wouldn't be because she really wanted him. It would be because she thought it was her duty. She would never see the kid as a real person. Her type never did. And Lenny was extremely vulnerable now, open to any cutting remark the society woman wanted to throw at him.

Hurt him, Miss Manners, he threatened silently, *and you'll have me to deal with.*

When there was another knock on his door, Sid shook himself loose from his irrationally violent anger.

"I'll get it," Lenny said, jumping up from his chair to pull open the door.

"I forgot—"

Sid rose slowly to his feet. The woman had stopped in the middle of a sentence and was staring at him. Which was only fair because Sid was very definitely staring at her. Her gleaming ash-blond hair skimmed her shoulders, making a perfect frame for creamy skin and pewter-gray eyes. Lowering his gaze, Sid discovered a body that was destined, he decided in that instant, to appear in quite a few of his future dreams, waking and sleeping.

"Hel-*lo*," he said, one thick brow raised. "What can I do for you? Want to buy an almost-new wedding ring? Looking to fence a hot vacuum cleaner?"

Lenny laughed. "This is Alyson."

Sid whistled softly through his teeth. So this was Miss Manners.

Alyson's eyes widened in blank surprise. "You're Sid the— You're Lenny's friend?"

When he nodded, she swallowed heavily. So much for her preconceived image. No stereotype ever drawn could describe this man. His plain brown shirt wasn't opened to the waist, and not one bit of gold decorated his neck or hands. The individual pieces of him—the brown hair and eyes, the prominent nose and strong jaw—on their own were all ordinary, but together they combined to make something far beyond ordinary. This was a supremely male male—masculinity without a drop of subtlety. He had a large muscular build, but he moved with ease, as though his mind knew well how to handle his powerful body. He looked out of place in an office, but she couldn't say where she would have placed him instead.

Maybe in a courtroom, behind the bench. Not that he looked like a judge. He didn't at all. But there was something in his eyes, something that said he had summed her up instantly and just as instantly found her wanting.

Glancing away from his watchful brown eyes, she looked around the small cluttered room and was visibly startled when her gaze connected with that of a dog with short brown hair. A very large, very angry dog. It seemed to be daring her to move, so it could rip off various and sundry body parts.

"Meet Grendel."

"Grendel?" She glanced back to the man still standing behind the desk. *"Beowulf?"*

"It's amazing what they put in Classic Comics, isn't it?"

Alyson choked back a spurt of laughter—she wasn't entirely sure he was making a joke—and kept her eyes on the dog. "So this is the monster who 'journeyed forever joyless,' " she murmured. "I can see the resemblance, poor thing."

" 'Hell's captive,' " Sid quoted softly. " 'That shadow of death hunted in darkness.' " When she turned toward him, he shrugged carelessly and added, "Grendel guards the place at night."

Rocking back on his heels, Sid fought to hide his irritation. She didn't have to look so shocked. As though his quoting *Beowulf* were some big deal. As though his being literate were some big deal. Sid had read the epic poem as a teenager, and when he found Grendel at the pound, when he had seen the tormented light in the dog's black eyes, the name seemed natural. The night he brought Grendel home, Sid had reread the tale. Several lines describing the monster had stuck. Maybe because they hit too close to home. Sid and Grendel were a lot alike. They were both restless souls, out of step with the rest of the world.

Smiling wryly, he glanced at the woman. Suddenly every muscle in his body tightened. On her face was a look he recognized instantly: *You're worthless, Sid.* It was there in her eyes, in her aloof features. *You're worthless, Sid.* He wanted to grab her and shake her until her perfect teeth rattled. He wanted to force her to see what was on the inside, force her to see that he was a man, not a piece of trash, damn her.

"So what can I do for you, Miss Ma— Miss Wilde?" he asked stiffly.

"Nothing. That is, I forgot to give Lenny any money." She grinned at the boy. "I can't believe you let me forget."

Lenny shrugged his thin shoulders. "I still have some of my allowance left."

"But today was supposed to be my treat." Her smile was strained now.

Sid had to give her credit. She was trying. "You don't have to worry about him when he's with me," he said. "Lenny's my pal. I'll take care of him."

Why had that make her angry? Sid wondered.

The pewter in her eyes had turned to steel, and her soft lips tightened.

"I'm sure you will," she said. "But Lenny's my responsibility, and I take all my responsibilities seriously."

"He's a boy, not a responsibility."

She drew in a sharp breath. "You know what I meant." After a moment she bit her lip. "Yes, he's a boy. And today is his day to visit old friends . . . so I'll get out of the way and let him get on with it."

If Sid read her right, today would be the last time Lenny would be visiting "old friends." He stood with fists clenched, jaw clamped shut, until she walked out of his office, then he sat down abruptly in his chair.

Snotty woman, he thought. Just who in hell did she think she was? Or, more to the point, just who in hell did she think he was?

It had been a long time since Sid felt as he did at this moment, as he had when he was a kid and nice girls wouldn't talk to him.

I hope you get yours someday, Miss Manners. I hope you get shaken out of that blue-blood composure, that smooth superiority that comes with being born rich. I hope someday you'll find out what it's like to be an ordinary human being.

And Sid hoped he'd be there when it happened.

Two

Alyson sat behind the small antique desk in her study. One of the blue ostrich feathers that dangled from the sequined headband on her forehead kept falling down, tickling her face. With the ornate headpiece—her thinking cap—Alsyon wore an orange University of Texas T-shirt, white clam diggers, and embroidered Oriental slippers.

On the desk in front of her were the plans for remodeling an old house in South Dallas. When it was finished, it would be the new Annabel Speary Home for Unwed Mothers, named for Alyson's maternal grandmother. Although it was her mother's project, Alyson was on the board of directors and was therefore involved in all stages of the planning.

It was a worthwhile cause, and Alyson had worked hard on the project, but somehow, tonight, it seemed dull.

Whine, whine, whine, she scolded herself silently.

Alyson was one of the lucky ones. She could do anything she wanted, without ever having to worry about money. Her two grandfathers had made enough money to last several lifetimes. There was no need for Alyson to worry about having a real home, her own home, either. Grandfather Wilde had built a huge monstrosity that could house half a dozen families. Alyson should have thanked her lucky stars that her parents had agreed to remodel the north wing for their only child's use. It gave her all the privacy she needed and was larger than any modern apartment she could have found.

"And if my hair were thirty-seven feet longer, I could be Rapunzel," she said, as she rose to her feet.

Swinging around, she ran to the leather couch and jumped up to the middle of it.

"Yo, Rapunzel," she called out. "Rappie-babe, drop your locks."

She flopped down and positioned her head on the padded arm of the couch so that her hair dropped over the end.

"I'm supposed to climb *that?*" she asked in the prince's deep voice. "Get real, chick."

Rolling over, she gave the prince a raspberry. No one liked a street-smart prince. A street-smart prince? Alyson had never conjured up that type of prince before, but the fact that she had now didn't surprise her. For three days she had heard echoes of the sneer in Sid Sweet's voice.

You're a boring, inconsequential woman, Miss

Wilde, and you lead a boring, inconsequential life, his eyes had told her. *You wouldn't know fun or adventure if it walked up and slapped you in the face.*

If Sid Sweet could see her in her fantasies, he wouldn't be so quick to judge. Since childhood, her dreams had been her best friends. In her dreams Alyson had been to Kuala Lumpur and Pago Pago; she had walked and talked with kings, and dined with primitive tribes. In her dreams she had been made love to by men from all over the world, exciting men who were excited by her. By *her.*

"In my dreams," she murmured, pulling herself up to sit cross-legged on the couch.

At twenty-six, Alyson had worn the title Spinster for at least five years. It wasn't that she was too old to begin a relationship. What counted was that everyone, even her parents, assumed that Alyson was too odd, just a bit too peculiar, to settle down to a normal life. Her childhood illnesses had set her apart, made her seem like a faded imitation of a living, breathing woman. And while she would give a mint to prove them all wrong, the fact was she *was* odd. She wanted excitement and adventure in her life. And the idea of marrying a nice acceptable man, one endorsed by her relatives, didn't thrill her. And to make matters worse, she felt she should be in love with her prospective husband.

She wanted a man as understanding as Blair and a child like Lenny. Her little cousin, with his sometimes blistering honesty, appealed to something deep and basic within her, and more than

once since he had come to live with her, she had
wished that he were her own child. Lenny had
had a tough life, but it hadn't broken him. And
he didn't have to fantasize adventures; he went
looking for them. Just as his father had done.
Just as Alyson had never had a chance to do.

She never talked about her fantasies. Not to
anyone. There was something a little sad about a
grown woman who needed dreams to fill her life.
The fantasies had begun when she was five, the
year Blair had come to them. Though her illness
had happened before then.

Her parents were loving people, but they were
also very busy. They hadn't thought of having
other children in to visit their daughter. The sole
inhabitants of Alyson's world were servants, doctors, physical therapists, tutors, and Blair. Especially Blair. Her only escape from the hated
confines of her bedroom were the fantasies she
and her cousin created. And the fictitious esca-
pades had become even more necessary when
Blair suddenly deserted her.

Although her cousin hadn't communicated
with her directly, over the years packages came
for her through the mail, exciting gifts from exciting places. When Blair settled down with Sandra,
the packages stopped coming. By that time
Alyson was almost recovered physically, but she
found herself unable to step back into the
ordinary world. So she began buying presents
for herself. She had African masks, Australian
boomerangs, South American bolos, and a lamp
whose base was a buxom brass woman with a
clock in her stomach. In an alcove in the sitting

room were three marble busts that had once belonged to Grandmother Speary. Aristotle wore a Peruvian hat; Socrates, an Afghan turban; and on Plato's head was a red cap with LOVE ME, LOVE MY TRUCK across the front.

Her apartment was now furnished with a mixture of antiques and exotic oddities. *Matching my personality perfectly*, she thought with a wry grimace.

Alyson was completely fit now. There were no traces of the delicate child she had been. No physical traces. But the fantasies were still there. They were her own silly way of wishing on a star.

My dear Alyson, I do believe you're going potty, she told herself.

"Going, going, gone," she muttered. Then, rising to her feet, she left the study.

When she opened the door to Lenny's bedroom, she took care not to let the light from the hall shine on his sleeping face. As usual, the boy's sleep wasn't peaceful. Lenny often had nightmares, but tonight seemed worse than usual. His face was covered with perspiration, and he was fighting the blanket as he muttered incomprehensibly urgent words.

Moving into the room, she placed a gentle hand on his shoulder. She didn't want to wake him, just to soothe him and let him know she was there.

Lenny's eyes flew open abruptly, and he stared at her for a moment before she saw him come fully awake. "Those feathers are just about shot," he said, reaching up to touch the headband. "Sheba ain't got nothin' on you. You been thinkin' again? You know that always gets you in trouble."

She stared at him silently, knowing his questions were simply an avoidance of hers. "Was it a bad one?" she asked softly.

He turned his head away from her. "I don't want to talk about it."

She sat down on the bed. "Lenny, this is not going to work."

He jerked his head back toward her, his eyes wide. "You gonna turn me over to the social workers now?"

"Dammit, Lenny," she said in exasperation, "get this through your thick head. *We are a family.* I will never willingly 'turn you over' to anyone."

"Because I'm your responsibility."

She wished to hell she had never used that word. Everyone seemed to want to jump on it. "Not just that. Your father was my best friend. I loved him. And believe it or not, I'm beginning to like his kid." She smiled. "You'll just have to face up to it. Whether you like it or not, you're stuck with me. When I said it wasn't going to work, I was talking about the way you keep shutting me out. Let me share whatever is bothering you. I promise it will help."

When the silence drew out, she was afraid he was going to ignore her, but seconds later Lenny began to speak.

"I was born in San León, you know about that. It's just a little town, and there's not much to do, no rich people or anything. Most of them had these little farms. But I liked it a lot. So did

Daddy. And I had a lot of friends there. Mercedes and Jacob—they were my best friends. Mercedes is the one who told me why all the people were so poor."

"What did she tell you?"

"She said all the good luck left town when somebody stole this statue from the church. It was a gold statue shaped like Mary."

"A Madonna."

"Yeah, that's what they called it. The 'Golden Madonna.' Anyway, ever since somebody stole it— it was a long, long time ago—San León just has bad luck. The sheep and goats don't have babies like they're supposed to, the bugs keep eating the stuff they grow on the farms. At least, I think it was bugs. It might have been birds or something. Anyway, Mercedes said it was all because this statue was gone."

"You realize that's just superstition?"

"Maybe," he said doubtfully. "But they all believe it. And if a lot of people believe something, it's almost like it's true."

"I guess so," she said. "Do you believe it?"

"I don't know." He paused. "What if somebody could get the statue back? What if somebody knew where it was and didn't tell them?"

She glanced away from him. Lenny was still not opening up to her. He was making idle talk to appease her. But, she told herself in resignation, any communication was better than nothing.

"That would be wrong," she said firmly. "Even if we discount the superstition attached to it, the Madonna belongs to the people in San León."

"And the person who knew and didn't tell—he'd

be scum, wouldn't he? He'd be pretty low." His voice was urgent and strangely condemning.

"Lenny, what is this all about? I thought you were just killing time until you fell asleep again, but you sound serious."

"I know," he whispered.

"You know what?"

"I know where the statue of Mary is. I saw it."

In halting words he told her how, six years earlier, he had gone camping with his father and two of their friends. They had made camp on top of a mesa, and one day, while the men hunted for fire wood, Lenny went exploring. That was when he found the Madonna. He stumbled upon a narrow crack in the earth and climbed down. Lenny wasn't able to reach the statuette because the way was blocked by fallen rock, but the sun was shining on it, and he saw it quite clearly.

Filled with excitement, Lenny hurried back to camp, anxious to tell his father what he had found. But he didn't get the chance. Blair had injured his head in a fall, and in the rush to get his father to the hospital a hundred miles away, Lenny forgot all about the Madonna. As the doctors worked on his father, the boy prayed that Blair would be all right. He prayed that God would take care of his father and make him well.

"But He didn't," Lenny said now, his voice uneven with emotion. "Daddy died. After that, after we left San León, I remembered the statue, but I didn't say anything."

"Why, Lenny?" she asked gently.

"Because I hated God. I *hated* Him. I didn't want the statue to go back to the church. Taking it back would be like helping God, and He didn't help my dad when I asked Him to. He didn't make Daddy get well."

"I'm so sorry, honey," she whispered. "I'm sorry you had to go through all that."

"Maybe. . . ," he whispered, "maybe that's why things are going bad now. It was all different before Daddy died. Mom, she would yell a lot, and sometimes she hit me, but Daddy would talk to her, and she'd tell me she was sorry. Then, after we left San León, she started drinking and taking pills to make her feel better. Sometimes she wouldn't come home for days at a time. And she'd leave me with people we hardly knew. I hated that. She'd go away with some guy and just forget I was there."

He wiped his eyes and stared at the ceiling. "But she always came back. Except this time. She isn't ever coming back. I could tell by the way she acted. Maybe if I hadn't hated God, if I'd have took the statue back, maybe none of it would've happened."

"You think God's punishing you?"

"Maybe."

"He's not," Alyson said vehemently, grasping his thin shoulders. "He doesn't work that way. He knows what's inside you. He knows you're hurting, and He would never do things that would hurt you more."

"Yeah," he whispered. "He knows what's inside me. He knows I'm rotten all the way down."

Alyson pulled him into her arms, and for a little while Lenny allowed the embrace. But only for a little while.

She didn't know what to tell him to make him understand that he wasn't a bad person, and since there was nothing she could say, she simply sat beside him until he fell into a restless sleep.

When she returned to the study, she found it impossible to concentrate on her work. She couldn't get her mind off Lenny. There was so much barely buried pain in him, and she was his only protection.

What a laugh, she thought. What a miserable little laugh. She was all Lenny had, and her life had become a mixture of commendable but detached good deeds and impossible illusions. What did she know about raising, protecting, and guiding a boy like Lenny?

When the doorbell rang, Alyson jumped and glanced at her watch. It was already ten-thirty, much too late for anyone she knew to be calling.

But apparently it wasn't too late for Sid Sweet. He stood on her doorstep, dressed all in black, as though he had been on a recent visit to the nether regions.

"The lady at the front door told me to come here," he said. "Are you being punished? How come they don't let you live with the rest of the family? Were they afraid Lenny would ruin the antiques with graffiti? What kind—"

He broke off and stared openly at her headband. "Just get back from a costume party?"

"It belonged to Grandmother Speary," she said, her voice distracted. "I use it for thinking."

"Right," he said, eyeing her warily. "I need to talk to you about Lenny. Do you know where he was today?"

"Of course I know," she said. Since Lenny was out of school for summer vacation, she had taken special pains to make sure his days were filled. "He went to a cookout at Chad Jennings's house. Chad's mother is a friend of mine, and I arranged for Lenny to be invited. He was there all day."

"Oh yeah? Chad doesn't wear a gold skull and crossbones earring, does he?"

She stared at him for a moment. "I think you'd better come in."

When they were both seated in the small sitting room, he glanced around, frowning as though he disapproved of the room as much as he disapproved of her.

"I don't usually fink on my friends," he said, reluctantly pulling his gaze away from the brass lamp, "but the guys Lenny's been hanging around with are trouble. They've been in and out of juvenile court more times than you can count." He paused. "I don't think Len's done anything illegal yet, but he will eventually. Sooner or later, he'll have to prove himself to the others."

She closed her eyes and exhaled slowly. "Where *was* Lenny today?"

"He took the bus back to my part of town. He didn't come in to see me—he knew I'd kick his butt if he did—but Sheba saw him with the gang. They call themselves the Brutes, a bunch of little punks trying to be bad. They're a weak-kneed pack—they don't make punks like they used to— but they're still not the kind of boys Len should be messing with."

"He wants to belong," she said, more to herself than to the man sitting across from her. "He wants to matter to someone. No, it's more than that. He needs to feel that his life has some value, that he can make a difference, even if it's in a negative way." She bit her lip. "I wish he could have taken the Madonna back. That would have shown him—"

"Madonna?" he interrupted. "I understood the psychological baloney, but you lost me on that one."

Alyson had forgotten he was there. Her first instinct was to keep quiet. She felt uneasy about discussing Lenny's private thoughts and feelings with a stranger, but this man obviously cared about Lenny. That alone gave him certain rights, so she used the next five minutes to tell him the story of the "Golden Madonna."

"I'm afraid for him, Mr. Sweet," she said finally, leaning forward in her chair. "If Lenny had been able to return the Madonna, he would have felt he'd done something really important in his life. He would have something to remember with pride, something he could hold onto during the bad times. It would have shown him that he had value, that he is a good person and his life makes a difference."

"It would show him that he's not worthless," he said quietly.

Alyson rose to her feet and walked to the window. Saying it aloud had only made it worse. It had made her feel even more impotent. If Blair had been there, he would have known how to help his son. Blair hadn't stayed at home, as she had. He hadn't dwindled into the family oddity. He had gone out and lived. And after his death, he'd left his son.

When he first arrived, Lenny had told Alyson all about his father's adventures. Before his marriage Blair had found his way to South American jungles and trekked through Soviet tundra. He had fought wars in Africa and crossed forbidden boundaries in the Far East.

And Alyson couldn't even manage to help a little boy find himself. But, sweet heaven, she wished she could. She wished she could take Lenny back to San León and help him find the Madonna. Even before the wish took shape, Alyson had a vision of herself in a white peasant dress, ammunition belts crisscrossing her chest as she fought the *banditos* who wanted the golden statue for themselves.

Not another fantasy! she screamed silently. This is real. This time mattered. Dreaming another stupid dream won't help Lenny.

But maybe it didn't have to be just a dream. There was nothing to prevent her from making the dream a reality. For Blair's son couldn't she manage to break loose, just this once?

"I'm going to do it," she whispered. "I'm really going to do it."

Exhilaration rushed through her. She was going to do it. The idea excited her, excited her more than anything since she had been a child. She was going to do something that wasn't neat and orderly. She was going to do something meaningful.

She was going to do something that would

make her parents have about nineteen seizures apiece, she thought wryly.

She swung around to face the man who now stood several feet from her. "Thank you for taking time to come here and tell me about Lenny. He's going to be all right. I'm going to make sure he's all right."

Alyson loved the way the confident words sounded in her mouth. She felt free, totally without restraint.

"How you figure on doing that?" Sid Sweet asked, his expression doubtful.

"We're going to go find Lenny's pride. We're going to San León to find the 'Golden Madonna' so he can take it back to where it belongs."

Sid Sweet laughed. He seemed to be trying to control it, but every time his gaze fell on her, he laughed even harder. In truth, he had a nice laugh. So nice that Alyson almost laughed with him. The only thing that stopped her was the fact that he was laughing at her.

"I know you think I'm pretty incompetent—"

"In the wilds of South Texas?" he said. "You'd better believe it. I've been down there. Civilization only occasionally visits. You won't find a chauffeured limo within three hundred miles."

"I wasn't thinking of taking Waldo with me," she said, distracted by the way he continued to stare at her. "I thought I would rent a car at the airport."

"Which airport is that?"

"The one at— Oh, I see. San León probably doesn't have an airport."

"San León probably doesn't have a traffic light," he said, his voice dry.

"Then I'll just have to—"

"Consult your travel agent?"

"—wing it," she finished airily.

He studied her face carefully. "You're really going to do this, aren't you?"

She nodded slowly. "It's important, Mr. Sweet. Lenny is mine now, and there are things I want for him." Lenny would have all the opportunities. Alyson wanted that for him. "Lenny will have his chance," she said with determination.

"The terrain will have changed in six years," he said quietly. "A lot."

"Yes," she admitted slowly. "It may take a while. I'll have to make sure we have enough food and . . . whatever."

" 'Whatever'? *Whatever*? Yeah, let's don't forget the whatever, for Pete's sake." He was staring at her as though she had gone mad. "You don't even know what you're doing. You don't even know how many things you don't know. And you're really going to do this?"

"Yes, I'm really going to do this," she said stubbornly. "And I must say I resent your attitude. You shouldn't judge people simply by appearance."

He snorted. "That's the pot calling the kettle black. Look, Miss Wilde, I don't care what kind of guts you've got. You're talking about going to the badlands. For that you've got to be tough inside and out. And, *judging by the outside*, your hide isn't tough enough for something like that."

Pushing a feather off her forehead, she glared

at him. "But then it's none of your business, is it? Lenny is my resp— Lenny is mine now. I'll do what I have to do to make things right for him."

He exhaled roughly, managing to put exasperation and animosity into the sound. "Judas priest, you're pig-headed. Why couldn't you have been your average, everyday socialite who would cart the kid off to a shrink to get his head straightened out?"

He swung away from her, walked a couple of steps, then turned to face her, his hands shoved in his pockets. "All right . . . all right. I guess I'll have to go with you. This is just exactly what I needed," he muttered under his breath. "Looking out for a couple of helpless crackpots."

"You want to go too?" she asked in surprise.

"I didn't say I wanted to. I said I guess I'll have to."

"Why?" she asked in genuine confusion. "Lenny said you never do anything that doesn't make a profit. He said— Oh. You mean you think there's more than the Madonna? You think the thieves who took the statue hid other things there as well, like a treasure trove?"

Alyson wouldn't mind finding a treasure trove. She had read about people locating sunken ships with fantastic cargoes and had fantasized about being in on the find. She didn't need the money, but discovering a lost cache would be exciting. It was certainly something to think about.

Sid almost laughed out loud when she'd inferred his reasons were motivated by profit. The only thing that stopped him was that his reason for going was probably even more laughable, more harebrained. He wanted to go because he liked Lenny and had, months earlier, made himself responsible for the kid. That was the admirable part. The not-so-admirable part was his desire to see little Miss Manners shaken up. He wanted to see her depending on him for survival. It would be supremely satisfying to make her realize he was a man who couldn't be dismissed with a haughty stare and a shrug of her elegant shoulders.

After a moment, he said, "Why not? If there is a treasure, you don't need it. Lenny doesn't because he has you. I, on the other hand, could always use the extra cash. And whether you want to admit it or not, you need me. I won't scare you with stories about wolves and rattlesnakes, but don't you ever read the newspaper? The world has gone a little crazy lately. Wouldn't a serial killer just love to find you and the boy out in a lonely place like that . . . all by yourselves?"

She frowned. "I hadn't thought of that."

When she glanced at him, Sid read open wariness in her gray eyes. As though she was having a tough time swallowing the idea of being alone with him in the wilds. As though she didn't trust a man like Sid Sweet.

Anger exploded inside him, and he moved a step closer to her. "You think I might take advantage of the situation? You think I might get out in the wilderness and be overcome by drooling, hell-formed lust?"

Before she could answer, he reached out, fingering the stray curls on her cheek, then moved his hand to cup her smooth neck. "It's definitely something to think about," he whispered roughly.

Alyson couldn't move. Something very strange was happening to her. She knew it couldn't have anything to do with the warm hard hand on her neck. It must be fear. That was it. She was paralyzed by fear, she decided, as a shiver of something that was definitely not fear shook through her.

"Yeah," he said. The word was a touch of warmth on her cheek. "It might be nice to see what a woman like you feels like. I've always wondered. Do you ever feel passion rip through you? And if it does, do you demand to be taken, or do you remember to say 'please' and 'thank you'? Does your body get all hot and wet when you make love"—he moved one hand across her shoulder—"or is it still cool and untouchable? Does your hair fall across your face, or does it stay all neat and tidy? These lips—are they ever swollen with kisses, or do they stay ever so firmly pursed?" He brushed his lips lightly across her. "Oh yeah, it just might be worth finding out."

Suddenly his hand dropped to his side, and he backed two paces away from her. "On the other hand, if I laid a finger on you, you'd send me packing, and I wouldn't get the treasure, would I?"

Alyson couldn't catch her breath. She stared at him in stunned silence. Her mind knew that nothing had really happened, but her body didn't believe it for a minute. She felt as though she should light up a cigarette and ask if it had been good for him too.

Swallowing an hysterical giggle, she inhaled deeply. "There—" she broke off and cleared her throat, "there's really no need for you to make fun of me. I wasn't thinking of you in that way." She shot a nervous glance in his direction. "You were just teasing, right?"

He shrugged. "Sure, I was just teasing."

"And you won't do it again?"

He slowly crossed his heart with his right index finger. "Cross my heart, hope to die, stick a needle in my eye," he said solemnly. "You want to spit on our palms and shake on it."

She had raised her palm to do just that before she realized he was teasing her again, so she simply extended her hand to seal the agreement.

He took her hand, but he didn't shake it. He cradled it in his as he stared down at her. "Let's hope we all find what we're looking for," he said slowly.

Three

On the flight to Del Rio, the first stop on the way to San León, Alyson sat in the middle seat. Neither of her companions was great company. Lenny had pressed his nose against the window at takeoff and hadn't removed it since; Sid Sweet had fallen asleep before the seat-belt signs went off. Grendel, the fourth member of their unorthodox company, had been sedated and was in the baggage compartment, presumably sleeping as soundly as his owner.

Despite Alyson's enthusiasm, Sid had organized the entire trip as well as purchased all their camping gear. Alyson had wanted to be involved in every part of the adventure, but Sid had quickly overruled her. He'd asked her a couple of simple questions, proving to both of them that she had no idea what they would need for the trip.

"You'd end up letting the salesman talk you

into buying a tent with three bedrooms, a garden kitchen, and a freakin' bidet," he told her.

While she was willing to admit she didn't know a lot about camping, his attitude was beginning to annoy the devil out of her. Everything about him was beginning to annoy the devil out of her.

"Lenny, are you stuck to the glass, or is someone out there on the wing?" she asked.

He turned to her and grinned. Lenny looked his normal surly-but-ready-to-enjoy-a-joke self, but Alyson glimpsed something just below the surface. There was a hint of wariness, as though he were afraid to let excitement take hold, as though he were afraid to believe it was really going to happen. Alyson knew how he felt. She was afraid too.

She had wanted to do something daring. She had wanted to live her life with spirit. She'd wanted *bold* and *plucky* to be her new bywords. She had gotten her wish. She was here, on a plane bound for adventure. But what if she couldn't hack it? What if she screwed up her chance and merely succeeded in letting Lenny down?

It couldn't happen, she told herself. She couldn't let it happen.

Glancing around, she saw that Sid was no longer asleep. His head still rested against the back of his seat, but he had turned toward her. He was watching her again, watching her with the dissecting look that set her nerves on edge.

"It looks like you're having second thoughts," he said, his voice husky from sleep.

She grimaced. "I had second thoughts about

two hours ago. I'm up to nineteenth or twentieth thoughts now. But not about taking Lenny to San León."

"About me?" The words were stiff, and so, abruptly, were his features.

"No . . . of course not," she said, staring at him in surprise. "You seem capable of handling anything that comes along. In that, I envy you."

He snorted, a loud, derisive sound. "Sure."

"You don't believe me? I guess that shouldn't surprise me. You take your strength for granted. Most aggressive people do. For you, this trip is not much more than an inconvenience. Just a small interruption of your life to help a friend." Her lips quirked in a slight smile. "We both know you're not looking for treasure. I suppose I owe you an apology for insinuating you were. I know you're here because you want to help Lenny. The thing is, you made the decision so casually, as if you were deciding to go to the store to buy some chicken soup for a friend. No big deal. To me, it *is* a big deal. To me, it's wild and scary and exciting. It's an outrageous undertaking. But you're the kind of person who does anything he wants— no qualms, no second thoughts."

"Nobody's like that," he said after a moment. "I mean, doing whatever they want to do. Everybody has some kind of unattainable goal." His lips twisted in a wry smile. "That old impossible dream we all just keep on dreaming."

For a moment he sounded mellow, approachable. Alyson shifted her position toward him. She pulled her knees up and leaned her head against the seat back as she examined his features.

"Tell me," she said. "Tell me about your dream. The thing you really wanted to do but couldn't."

Sid studied the earnest interest in her gray eyes. *I want to kiss you,* he thought. *I want that real bad.*

The urge was unexpected. Although she was beautiful enough to stir any man's interest, she wasn't his type. In fact, she was the type he hated most. No, that was wrong. Originally, at their first meeting, he had shoved her in a pigeonhole labeled MRS. BARTLETT, just another rich princess who got her kicks from stepping on the underdogs. But that night, at her place, he had had second thoughts. That night he had seen something quirky in her nature—that silly feathered headband; the absurdly whimsical way she had decorated her home—and he had found himself intrigued. He had glimpsed something in her that had surprised him. A concealed but distinct vulnerability that made him want to hold her and tell her not to worry, because everything would be okay.

Which was crazy, he told himself in irritation. She didn't need Sid Sweet's reassurances. She was one of the chosen. One of the privileged who always ended up with the odds on their side. And vulnerable or not, he wasn't about to keep her entertained by exposing his past failures, his past heartaches. Or his thwarted dreams.

"I wanted to join the Peace Corps," he said. His indifferent statement broke the long silence. "The fact that I couldn't didn't exactly throw me into a deep dark depression, but it's something I wanted to do but couldn't."

"Why?"

He raised one brow. "*Which* why? Why did I want to join? Or why didn't I go into a depression because I couldn't?"

"No, I mean why couldn't you join?"

His lips tightened. "That's a stupid question— No, on second thought, maybe it's not. You said strong people take their strength for granted. Well, upper-class people do the same with their privileges."

She frowned. "You have to be rich to join the Peace Corps? When did they make that rule?"

She looked genuinely confused, and it irritated the hell out of him. He exhaled slowly. "Let me try to explain this. It's not about official restrictions. It's about expectations. About someone's personal range of possibilities." When she still looked bewildered, he said, "What did you grow up expecting to do after high school? I don't mean what you wanted to do. I mean what did you *expect* to do?"

"Go to college, of course."

" 'Of course,' " he mimicked sourly. "In my crowd the highest expectation I can remember was this one guy, Toni French, who wanted to work for the telephone company. Most of the guys just hoped they could get a job with some security, a job that would give them a shot at making foreman someday. College wasn't even a consideration. It wasn't in their personal range of possibilities. Or mine. The girls I knew expected to get married and have half a dozen kids by the time they were thirty. For me, the Peace Corps was like one of those girls dreaming of marrying Donald Trump. That kind of thing doesn't happen to people like us."

"I'm sorry. I still don't understand. I mean, I do about the Donald Trump part. Those girls probably wouldn't get a chance to mix with his crowd, but anyone can join the Peace Corps."

"And anyone can grow up to be president," he said, his voice cutting. "How many kids living in the slums really believe that? It's a nice thing to say, but it's not real. Things like joining the Peace Corps, going to college, being a movie star—those things are impossible for some people. No one ever told them, no one ever showed them by example, that they were anything but establishment hype."

Alyson listened carefully, and she tried to understand, but it was no use. She heard the anger in his voice, the same frustrated anger she had seen in him before, but she was no closer to understanding it now than she had ever been.

He was so strong, so sure of himself. How could anything as simple as joining the Peace Corps be a problem?

Expectations. Range of possibilities.

In her second year in college Alyson had gotten to know a group of freewheeling young people. One day they decided to leave college and go hitchhiking across Europe. They wanted to experience life firsthand, they told her, and they wanted Alyson to go with them. Alyson hadn't even considered it. She had dreamed about it.

She had built fantasies around the idea, but she hadn't considered it a real possibility. Rebelling had been outside her personal range of possibilities.

"I think I understand," she said slowly. "But you're different from the people you grew up with. You didn't get a job that would give you a shot at making foreman someday. You have your own business."

"I got smarter," he said abruptly. "I found out you can expand your expectations. In some cases. I had to learn the hard way that for some people, some things will always be out of their reach."

Was he talking about himself, or was this his way of suggesting that her part in this adventure was ludicrous because she would never, not in a million years, measure up?

The thought depressed her, but she fought against it. Before this trip was over, she would more than likely run into worse things than Sid Sweet's disapproval. She couldn't give up before she had even begun.

I can do this, she told herself. She would expand her expectations. There were no restraints other than the ones she put on herself. Anything was possible.

"We're landing," Lenny said at that moment.

Alyson picked up the boy's hand and squeezed it. Anything was possible.

Dressed in only a short zebra-striped silk slip, Alyson groaned and leaned her forehead against the full-length mirror in the bathroom of her hotel room.

She was tired. Every drop of boldness and pluck had drained out of her, and her range of possibilities seemed to have shrunk in direct proportion to her energy.

Sid and Lenny's rooms were on the same floor. They had promised to pick her up on their way down to dinner. Tonight they would have a decent meal and get a good night's sleep. Tomorrow they'd drive to San León.

She should be even more excited than when she had first made the decision, but she wasn't. It was her adventure, for heaven's sake. Why did she feel as though it were going on without her?

"Sid Sweet," she muttered, answering her own question as she turned away from the mirror.

Sid Sweet's unyielding, supercritical regard was the reason she didn't want to leave her room. He made her feel awkward, off balance. He was always watching her, studying her with that so-lazy sensuality in his drooping eyelids. Not that he thought of her in a sexual way, she told herself wryly. The sensuality was in him and would be there, no matter whom he happened to be looking at.

Wandering through the open door to the small balcony, she exhaled a slow breath. It was strange. Really strange. She had spent a lot of time kicking herself for not being the woman she wanted to be, but now that Sid Sweet was silently sending the same message, *constantly* sending it, she felt defensive. What right did he have to think as badly of her as she did of herself?

When she glanced up, Alyson saw a small plump woman three balconies away, watching her, staring openly at the flimsy zebra-striped slip.

Alyson turned toward the French doors, then stopped abruptly. "I'm only going in because I *want* to go in," she called out to the baffled woman.

"This is good," Alyson murmured as she walked back into her room. "Anger is good."

The anger invigorated her. It strengthened her. Jumping up on the bed, she stood in the middle and laughed aloud. She could get used to the feeling. Next time he looked at her with that look in his dark brown eyes, she wouldn't politely withdraw from combat. She would stand up to him. She would look him straight in the eye and say—

"Miss Wilde . . . Alyson." The voice came through the door as she heard the knock. It was Sid.

Swinging around, Alyson walked to the headboard and leaned her forehead against the wall. After a moment she drew her head back and banged it once, then twice, on the wall, trying to force her grit to resurface. When it didn't, she said, "Yes?" her voice tentative.

There was a drawn-out moment of silence. Then he said, "You want to open the door so we don't have to stand here yelling back and forth?"

"Noooo," she said to the wall, "I don't think so."

"What? I can't hear you. Is something wrong?"

She cleared her throat. "I've decided to skip dinner tonight," she called out, her voice doggedly nonchalant. "See you both tomorrow."

Another silence. "Why don't you want to open the door? You sound strange."

"I'm tired . . . flying always makes me tired. See you tomorrow," she yelled again.

The sound of muffled voices came from the hall, but seconds later they dwindled, then disappeared. Turning away from the wall, she sat down heavily on the mattress.

After a moment she reached up and thumped herself on the forehead with her index finger. "You have the backbone of a *Slinky*," she groaned, then crossed her legs and leaned forward until her forehead touched the bed.

In her dreams. Only in daydreams could she be forceful and confident. Standing up to a man like Sid Sweet was as wild a fantasy as climbing Mt. Everest.

"Is this some kind of rich people's ritual, or are you meditating?"

The deep husky voice came from the balcony. It was real. At least she was pretty sure it was real. She didn't sit up. Her head was still pressed to the bed when she swiveled it to the side and slowly opened her eyes. Sid Sweet stood in the doorway leading from the balcony, one thick brow arched as he stared at her.

A choked sound escaped her as she scrambled to her feet. Grabbing the bedspread, she pulled at it frantically, but since she was standing on it, she succeeded merely in hopping around frantically, trying to step off it and cover herself with it at the same time.

"Is this another part of the ritual?" he asked. "Is it going to start raining money now?"

Alyson had managed to pull up one little corner of the spread and now held it clutched to her breasts. But glancing down, she saw the corner didn't cover anything. It just looked ridiculous.

Dropping the spread with a sigh, she turned to lean her hips against the wooden headboard. "What are you doing here? People aren't supposed to go hopping onto balconies that don't belong to them."

"You bought the hotel?"

"You know what I mean. I've paid for the use of that balcony tonight, and you're not supposed to be on it."

"Have I committed a breach of etiquette?" he asked, then gave a short harsh laugh. "I think you must have mistaken me for a gentleman. *Gentlemen* don't hop onto the wrong balcony. *Gentlemen* don't stare at nice girls when they catch them wearing sexy little slips. Gentlemen don't. But *men* do."

That distant, mocking tone was back in his voice, and once again Alyson didn't know how to respond to it.

She moistened her lips. "Did you want something, Mr. Sweet?"

He threw back his head and laughed, this time in genuine amusement, as he moved into the room. "Yeah . . . yeah, there's something I want. I want you to take off that silly little slip, *this second*, so I can see the rest of your body. I want to throw you down on the bed and eat you up. I want to touch you and kiss you until you squeal uncle. I want to roll on top of you and fill . . . you

. . . up." He paused and smiled. "That's what I want, Miss Wilde."

When he reached the foot of the bed, he stopped talking. He simply stood there, as though waiting for an answer.

Alyson pressed one damp palm to her chest in a futile attempt trying to still her thudding heart. After a moment she moistened her lips. "Isn't Lenny waiting down—" she began. Then realization dawned. "Oh, I see. You're teasing me again. Why did you really come here?"

The intense regard, the tension in his broad shoulders, eased slightly. "Lenny was worried about you."

"Did he say that?" In order to worry, one had to care. Was it possible Lenny was beginning to like her? "Did he say he was worried about me?"

"I think his exact words were 'She flips out ever' once in a while. I mean, she gets these weird moods.' "

"So you came to check up on me?" she asked hesitantly.

He shrugged. "You didn't sound like you were going to open the door anytime soon."

Pushing away from the headboard, she stepped off the bed. "I'll come down if it will make Lenny happy, but I don't see why you couldn't have used the telephone."

He was silent, watching her with the same look in his brown eyes that had been there since their first meeting.

"Will you stop looking at me like that?" she snapped in exasperation. "I have a perfect right to be annoyed. You came bursting in here, scaring the wits out of me, making little jokes in that charmingly reptilian way of yours. At my expense. Just who do you think you are?"

Before she could blink, he reached out, grasped her arm, and pulled her body closer, letting her feel the heat of his anger.

"Sid Sweet," he said, his voice tight and rough. "Got that? I'm Sid Sweet. A human being. The way I figure it, that gives me just as many rights as you."

She jerked away from him, rubbing the red spot on her arm. "*Just* as many," she agreed, keeping her voice calm with effort. "Do you see me hopping around on *your* balcony?"

He gave a short bark of laughter, then turned and walked to the door that led to the hall. "Lady, my imagination isn't that good."

Raising her chin, she followed him. "I could. If I wanted to, I could do it."

"Sure you could." He opened the door and stepped into the hall. "I'll leave the balcony door open for you."

"You do that!" she yelled as the door swung shut behind him. "You— You just do that," she said, her voice dwindling away.

She stood for a moment, glaring at the door, then turned away, and suddenly, startlingly, laughter rose in her throat. The whole scene had been ridiculous, and exciting. This was the exhilaration, the emphatic verve, her life had been missing. Who would have thought Sid Sweet would be the one to bring it to her?

"I love it, I love it, I love it," she said as she

jumped back onto the bed and hopped off the other side to pull open the closet door.

She put on the only thing she had brought with her that was suitable for dining in the hotel—a short black taffeta skirt, made even fuller by a rustling black-net petticoat, and an emerald-green long-sleeved blouse, its wide lapels coming together in a deep V between her breasts. Confident clothes for a suddenly confident woman.

Alyson was still smiling when she walked into the dining room fifteen minutes later. It was soon apparent, however, that Sid Sweet didn't share her good humor. He remained stone-faced and silent throughout the meal. Only once did he address a comment to her.

"For Pete's sake, my name is Sid," he snapped at her. "It's not a real, complicated name. Sid. S–I–D. So will you cut out the 'Mr. Sweet' business?"

His mood went downhill after that.

Sid lay on the bed, his eyes wide open, even though the room was dark. He had been lying there, wide awake, for hours, brooding about dinner. And about her.

She had known he was uncomfortable in the high-class hotel restaurant. And she had enjoyed his discomfort. That much had been obvious. All evening she had grinned like a cat playing with a mouse.

That was all right, he told himself. She might be in her element here—in the elegant hotel she had chosen instead of a Holiday Inn, like any ordinary human being would have—but just wait until they got out in no-man's-land. They would see who came out on top then. In the badlands it would be Sid's turn to laugh.

He shifted his position when he heard laughter and music from the room next door. It wasn't her room of course. It was the one on the other side. The people there had been partying big-time for several hours, and if he had been in a motel, Sid would have pounded on the wall, but somehow that didn't seem like the thing to do in this place.

Seconds later, when he heard a muffled but distinct noise on the balcony, *his* balcony, he sat up in irritation. Enough was enough. If the inconsiderate idiots had moved the party outside, he might just decide to chuck a couple of them over the railing.

As soon as he opened the French doors, he saw someone hanging—half-on, half-off his balcony.

"What in hell do you think you're doing?" he growled.

"Don't help."

He recognized the voice immediately, even though it was strained from the balcony rail pressing into her abdomen. She teetered for a moment, then slid head first onto the balcony floor, black-net petticoat covering everything but what it was supposed to cover.

Fighting the stiff net, she finally managed to surface long enough to say, "I told you I could do it."

"What in hell do you think you're doing?" he repeated.

She stood up, brushed down her skirt, and

straightened her blouse. "I should think that's perfectly obvious. I'm hopping around—" She broke off and stared at him. "You're naked. You—You're stark naked."

"As stark as they come," he agreed, his tone unconcerned as he leaned against the wall.

"Oh, dear," she whispered.

He smiled, savoring the moment. "Isn't this an interesting development?" he said slowly. "When we were in your room, you saw how a man, as opposed to a gentleman, reacts to a . . . a delicate situation. Now it's my turn. Let's see how you react, Miss Wilde. Like a lady. Or a woman."

Alyson stood in the corner of the balcony, holding on to the rail for dear life. What did he expect her to do? What did he *want* her to do? She had no hope of reading him. The only thing she could do was be herself.

"You— You have a very nice body, Mr. . . . Sid."

He studied her face so intently, Alyson shifted in embarrassment. "Well, what's the verdict?" she asked shortly. "You *are* judging me, aren't you? You've been doing it since the minute we met. Suffice it to say it makes me extremely uncomfortable."

"Consider it sufficed," he drawled lazily.

"Why do you do that?" She stepped away from the railing. "Do you treat everyone like this? Or do you save it for women? Actually, I don't think it's either. I think it's me. I think you treat me different." She paused, biting her lip. "While I'll admit I deserve—"

"You *deserve*?" he broke in sharply. "You *deserve*? From people who care about status, from people who really give a damn, you may deserve reverence, honor, and brownnosing to the nth degree. From me, someone who just doesn't give a flying fig, you deserve only what you damn well *earn*!"

She was shivering, shaking violently from the force of the words he'd thrown at her. She always shook when she was caught in a confrontation. But this time there was a difference. She wasn't running. She wasn't even shrinking inside.

Drawing in a deep breath, she raised her chin. "I can live with that," she said quietly.

He laughed. It was deep rumbling laughter that made her lips twitch in answering amusement.

"You'll have to. At least until this trip is over." He paused to study her features. "I have to say this for you. You can throw some surprises at me." He began to move slowly toward her. "I guess what surprises me most is that you can surprise me. I didn't expect that. On the outside you're just a little too perfect, a little too poised and a little too beautiful. But you've got something inside you. Radical stuff—offbeat and unpredictable."

His voice had deepened as he drew closer. "You really like my body?" he whispered roughly.

She gave one short nod. It was all she could manage. He was too close. He had backed her into the corner and deprived her of room— room for thinking, room for reasoning, room for breathing.

"Is that an impartial opinion?" he murmured,

reaching out to thread his fingers through her hair and cup her neck. "Is it something like saying 'that's a nice chair,' or 'that's a good-looking car'?"

Impartial? She had never felt less impartial in her life. In the past few minutes she had become overwhelmingly partial to this particular body and the way it gleamed like molten gold in the moonlight.

She could see it, every inch of it, all too clearly, and her imagination, the thing that had saved her sanity as a child, kicked into overdrive. She knew, as she let her gaze drift over his bare flesh, what it would be like to have that flesh pressed against hers. Sweet heaven, she could *feel* it. When his smooth muscled chest rose and fell with his breathing, she felt the movement. When he took another step toward her, his hard thighs flexed, and she felt them flexing against her.

Incredible heat grew in the center of her, spreading outward, reaching every inch of her body. She was burning up. She was standing on a strange balcony in a strange city, and she was burning up. Before long the heat would consume her, and she would be nothing more than a pile of ashes. It wasn't a fate she had ever imagined for herself, but she would have fought anyone who tried to put out the fire.

Raising her head, she met his eyes and saw she wasn't the only one on fire. And this time the fires in his brown eyes had nothing to do with anger. As crazy as it sounded, he was as affected by her as she was by him. He wanted her, the same way she wanted him. He couldn't deny it, even if he tried. The moonlight was her witness.

When he moved a stiff, awkward step closer, Alyson caught her breath and waited, anticipation and desire making the hair on her arms stand on end.

Then he seemed to catch himself, and his features went abruptly blank, the fires extinguished. He let out a slow rough breath, ran his fingers through his hair, then, incredibly, threw a nonchalant arm around her shoulders.

She hated him for that damned nonchalance.

"Come on, Princess," he said roughly. "Time to see if you can find that pea under the mattress."

His mattress? But no, pausing just long enough to pull on his Levi's, he opened the door to the hall for her.

"One thing," he said as she passed him.

"Yes?"

"What I said before about deserving only what you earn? That goes both ways. Lay off the attitude when you talk to me, when you look at me. You don't know a thing about me."

She met his eyes. "Will I? Ever?"

"Oh, yeah," he said tightly. "You'll know me. You can make book on it."

Four

Alyson inspected the bureau drawers and the closet for the third time, reassuring herself that she had packed everything. She glanced at her watch, then walked into the bathroom to check her appearance. For the third time.

Today she wore a short-sleeved jungle-print shirt with khaki pants, and her hair was pulled back with a mother-of-pearl clip. "Nothing has fallen apart in the last five minutes," she muttered, glancing again at her watch.

Maybe she had misunderstood. Maybe they weren't going to pick her up on their way down. Or maybe they had stopped by while she was in the shower.

Leaving the room, she walked past Sid's to reach the one Lenny occupied. When she knocked on the door, the boy opened it immediately.

"I was afraid you had already gone down," she said. "Are you ready for breakfast?"

He shrugged his thin shoulders. "Whatever."

"Once again, your enthusiasm leaves me breathless. Should we stop by Mr.— Sid's room?"

Lenny stopped chewing on his fingernail long enough to cut his eyes toward her. "I don't think so."

"Has he gone down already?"

"Uh-uh."

Alyson grabbed his thin shoulders and turned him to face her. "Raise your eyes. That's right, all the way to my face. Now, just for a moment, remove your hand from your mouth." She smiled when he blinked and did as he was told. "Okay, ready? This is going to be a tough one for you, Lenny. I want you to communicate. Com-mun-i-cate. Speak to me. Reveal the secrets hidden in your labyrinthine mind. Lay a couple of thoughts on me, O Silent One."

He stared at her for a moment before his lips twisted in a reluctant grin. "Like what?"

"Like why are we not going to stop by Sid's room? Like why did you act so mysterious when I asked you about stopping by his room?"

This time, when he shrugged, Alyson was ready for him, and they shrugged simultaneously. Lenny almost laughed. "I called him up a minute ago," he said. "He kept saying, like he had a mouthful of cotton or something, he kept saying, 'Go away, go away.' Now can we go eat?"

She frowned. "Maybe he's ill. Did he sound ill?"

"No, he sounded hungover . . . big time."

She blinked in surprise. Sid had been perfectly sober when she had left him the night before. Had he sat alone in his room, drinking enough to have a raging hangover this morning? Or had he brought someone into his bedroom for a little private party?

None of my business, she told herself firmly. He was a grown man and certainly didn't have to answer to her. Nonetheless, as she and Lenny ate breakfast, she wondered. And as she wondered, her imagination—her wonderfully vivid imagination—worked overtime.

Lenny dropped his napkin beside his plate and stood up. "It'll probably be a few hours before Sid gets his brain back in gear. I'm going to find the game room."

"Hours?" she repeated, frowning. "Wait, Lenny. If we have free time, we could do some sightseeing. Doesn't that sound like fun? The brochures in the room show some fantastic aboriginal cave paintings in this area."

Lenny rolled his eyes.

"Or . . ." she said slowly, "or we could go across the border to Ciudad Acuna."

He shifted his feet, looking bored.

"I've got it," she said. "Judge Roy Bean's grave. We could go see where Judge Roy Bean is buried."

"What does it do?"

She drew her head back, raising a questioning brow as she stared at him. "What do you mean, 'What does it do?' What is it supposed to do?"

"I don't know, but why would anybody but a total suck-up want to see a ratty old judge's grave unless a skeleton pops up or something?"

"It's history. Not just Texas history. This is a relic from the Wild West. It's—" She broke off and sighed. "Right. Why would anyone but a total suck-up want to see a ratty old judge's grave? Okay, you win. Go find the game room. But Lenny—" she placed a hand on his arm to make sure he was paying attention "—just the game room, okay? I don't want you to leave the hotel."

He shrugged, said, "Whatever," and left.

Alyson sat for a while, playing with a piece of cold toast, then stood up abruptly and picked up the check. Minutes later she stepped off the elevator on the fourth floor and walked to Sid's room. Her first knock was hesitant. Her fifth was determined. By the time she got to the tenth, her knock was vehement, forceful, and loud.

"Go away!" The bellowed words came from inside the room.

"Mr. Sweet," she called through the door, "talking to me for a few minutes is going to exacerbate your headache a lot less than my banging on the door for the rest of the—"

The door swung open. *"What?"*

The man could certainly put a wealth of meaning into a little one-syllable word. His chest and feet were bare, the snap on his jeans undone. His brown hair was rumpled, his eyes bloodshot, and his complexion a sickly shade of gray. It was definitely a hangover.

"I need to talk to you about Lenny," she said.

"And it couldn't wait until my head shrinks back to normal size?"

She shook her head. "This may be our last chance to be alone."

"I never pass up a chance to be alone with a beautiful woman." Moving to the side, he waved her in. "Come in . . . strip down . . . hop into bed . . . let's party," he said, his voice toneless.

The other times he had teased her about sex, he had been wickedly taunting. This time he acted as though he found the sound of his own voice painful.

Gingerly closing the door, he walked across the room and eased his body down to sit on the bed.

"So talk," he said.

In the coffee shop she had felt resolute, even aggressive, but she must have used up all her aggression on the door because now she couldn't quite remember all the things she had felt moved to tell him.

"Lenny looks up to you," she said finally. "At first, before I met you, that worried me quite a lot. You have to admit some of the things you told him were rather cynical. But then I came to understand you cared about Lenny, you cared about what happened to him. And I realized you were actually trying to teach him—"

"In my own reptilian way?" he inserted dryly.

She arched one slender brow in surprise. "Did that bother you? I was simply trying to, you know, get into the spirit of the thing."

" 'Get into the spirit of the thing'?" he repeated slowly. "You were trying to get into the spirit of the thing? You act like it was a game."

"Wasn't it?" Her lips tightened. "Every time we're in the same room, you begin an argument. I assumed you did it for recreation."

He rose to his feet, abruptly. "*Judas priest*, I hate it when you talk in that prissy-proper, good-little-girl way of yours!" Cradling his head between his open palms, he closed his eyes and groaned, "Judas priest, I hate it when I yell."

Regaining his seat, he said, "Maybe you're right. Maybe I do start a fight every time we're together. That's the only time you act like a real human being."

"I didn't come here so you could add to my list of faults," she said. "I came to talk about Lenny." She paused. "You made me forget where I was."

"You had decided I wasn't quite as scummy as you first thought because I care about Lenny."

"I don't think that's quite what I said." She met his gaze. "You do care about him, don't you?"

He shrugged in a Lennylike way. "He's not a bad kid. Are we getting close to the point of this discussion?"

She cleared her throat and glanced away from the growing annoyance in his eyes. "I don't know how much you know about Lenny's background—"

"I met his mother. What else do I need to know?"

"Yes, well, then you'll understand that because of his mother, he has come to view certain behavior as normal, behavior that I would rather he regarded as unacceptable." She moistened her lips in a nervous gesture. "Mr. Sweet . . . Sid, I know I have no right to— That is, normally I wouldn't consider it any of my business how you—"

"For sweet Pete's sake, spit it out!"

When they both flinched at the shouted words, Alyson almost laughed.

"Lenny knew immediately that you had had too

much to drink last night," she said after a moment. "I *hate* it that he recognized the symptoms so readily. You can't do this anymore." She met his eyes. "Not while we're on this trip. Not while you're around Lenny."

Color darkened his face. His eyes narrowed, and his nostrils flared. "You're going to tell me what to do?" His voice was deadly calm. "You're going to tell *me* what to do?"

"Well, I—"

He jumped to his feet. "You've got some nerve. You've never done a day's work in your life." He took a step toward her. "You've never had a problem that Mummy and Daddy couldn't fix for you." This time, when he took a step toward her, she moved a step back. "You've never had a heartache that your inherited money couldn't soothe away. And you're going to tell *me* how to live my life? Get real." He jabbed her in the shoulder with one finger. "Get freakin' real!"

Alyson swallowed heavily. "You're making a lot of assumptions when you don't even know me."

"Right. And you don't know me."

"And we're back where we started," she muttered, turning away.

She hadn't even taken the first step when he caught her by the shoulder and swung her back to face him. "I thought I told you last night— Oh, what the hell," he muttered as he pulled her into his arms.

She knew as soon as his arms closed around her that she had been waiting for the kiss. Not the little butterfly caress he had teased her with that night in her sitting room. She had been waiting for a real kiss.

This one was real, all right. Rough and hard and real. His fingers bit into her waist; his hips pressed her against the door, his lips grinding into hers. The fury of it shocked her, but it didn't take her long to adjust. Not long at all. Her emotions simply picked up where they had left off the night before.

Instant passion—simply add two lips, she thought as she dug urgent fingers into his biceps and opened her mouth to accept everything he had to give.

Without warning he jerked away from her. Moving a step back, his eyes widened as though he had received a shock. He glanced away, wiped his mouth on his forearm, then looked at her again, his eyes still wide and startled.

"What's with you?" The words were ragged. "What kind of woman doesn't even know an insult when somebody throws one at her?"

"Was—" she swallowed heavily, "was that what it was?" Blinking away the pain, she touched her mouth with one finger. "Maybe next time I'll recognize it." She drew herself up straighter, avoiding his eyes. "But then again, maybe I won't. Just to be on the safe side, you might consider not throwing any more insults my way."

She turned and opened the door, pausing to look over her shoulder at him. He hadn't moved. His stunned expression hadn't changed. "What does heartache have to do with your getting drunk last night?"

The question seemed to startle him. He stared

at her for a moment, then shook his head. "Nothing. I just started yelling. I had no idea what words were going to come out."

"I see." She walked out, closing the door softly behind her.

Sid stared at the door for a long time after she had gone, waiting for his heart to stop racing, waiting for his body to stop throbbing, waiting for the backwash, the aftermath of being close to her, to subside.

It was all his own stupid fault. He had thought he could get rid of her, override her accusations, if he showed contempt. But when she had melted in his arms, when she had responded to him, the contempt got lost somewhere. And for the life of him, he couldn't find it again. He couldn't find anything but aching need.

Turning, he caught a glimpse of his image in the mirror—the unkempt hair, the bloodshot eyes—and grimaced in distaste. She was right. He was a pig for letting Lenny know he had a hangover. He was a pig for getting drunk in the first place.

After she had left the night before, he had tried to relax enough to fall asleep, but it was a lost cause. He kept seeing the look in her eyes, eyes that had turned to silver in the moonlight as she stared at his body. Each time the memory returned, his muscles tightened in response. It happened over and over again. He couldn't get the sight of her, the feel and smell of her, out of his mind.

After a couple of hours, in self-defense, he left the hotel and headed across the border to Ciudad Acuna. He had no purpose in mind. He only knew that if he wanted to stay sane, he had to get away from the hotel. Away from her.

In Acuna he had found a lot of bars and a lot of women. Ready women. Women willing to do anything with anyone. For a price. As he shook his head at one smiling proposition after another, he suddenly heard a voice inside his head. *This is the type of love you deserve,* it said to him.

He didn't know where the thought came from, but it left him in shock. He had honestly believed he had worked through all that. He believed he had gotten rid of all the old feelings of self-contempt.

But he hadn't. The feelings had been there all along. They had been just below the surface, waiting for someone to come along and exhume them. Someone like Alyson.

That was when Sid began to drink.

Alyson stared in determination at the video screen in front of her. "The mushroom, Lenny! What did you tell me about the mushroom?"

"Eat it," Lenny said, his voice blunt. "It makes you more powerful."

She glanced at him. "That doesn't sound like a real smart message to get across to kids—see a strange mushroom and eat it because it will make you more powerful."

Lenny shrugged. "Doesn't matter now. You're dead."

She turned her head back to the screen. "But that's not fair. I wasn't through."

"That's life," he said, grinning as he moved her aside to take his turn at the game.

When she had joined him in the game room, Lenny hadn't welcomed her with open arms, but he hadn't chased her out with a stick either.

Things were looking up, she thought wryly.

She had made a fool of herself in Sid's room. There was no getting around it. She had definitely made a fool of herself. Alyson wasn't a judgmental sort of person. As a result of being far from perfect herself, she was willing to forgive a lot of things. But she didn't know if she could ever forgive Sid for witnessing her foolishness.

"Hello."

She glanced around sharply and saw him standing close behind her. He didn't look like the same man she had left only an hour earlier. His hair was still damp from the shower, and his complexion had lost its grayness.

After a moment he dropped his gaze to her lips. They were barely swollen, but now they began to throb, as though his gaze were a physical touch.

As he studied her, his firm lips twisted in an unamused smile. "I—" He broke off abruptly and shoved his hands in the back pockets of his jeans. "Truce?"

The word was short and unemotional, but there was something in his eyes, something wary and diffident.

She exhaled slowly. "Sure, why not?"

He didn't smile, but she could almost feel the tension in his stiffly held shoulders ease.

Lenny, his game over, moved away from the screen and turned his attention to a fingernail that needed chewing.

Sid smiled at the boy. "Okay, guys, ready to roll?"

Lenny glanced at Alyson, and, in unison, they shrugged their shoulders and said, "Whatever."

Five

According to the sign at the edge of town, San León was home to seven hundred and five people, but it was a very old sign. A few hundred could have moved in—or out—since it had been painted.

Lenny had said his hometown was poor, but through some mysterious mental process Alyson had translated that to mean the town was small and quaint and loaded with atmosphere. It *was* small. And since every town had some sort of atmosphere, she supposed San León had atmosphere, but it was of the gritty, dusty kind.

The narrow buildings lining the town's main street had been built in the plain, bare architectural style popular at the turn of the century. Sagging wooden awnings provided shade for cracked cement sidewalks. Weeds grew high in dirt alleys. Several plastic planters filled with sun-singed marigolds had been placed along the sidewalk in an abortive attempt to brighten the surroundings.

"We're here," Alyson said warily, breaking the silence that had fallen in the car.

"It's ugly," Lenny said abruptly.

She bit her lip when she heard the disappointment in his voice. Because the town held special memories for him, he had built it up in his imagination. As she knew from personal experience, reality rarely matched what was produced in the mind. She had turned in the seat, ready to reassure Lenny when Sid spoke.

"You got that right. It's damn sure ugly."

Alyson could have kicked him. Lenny needed to hear something positive, something that would dilute his disappointment. Sid glanced at her, his eyes gleaming with enjoyment when he saw the anger in her features.

"It's ugly," he continued, "and it's not even very friendly-looking." He smiled. "Kind of like Grendel back there."

The dog rode behind the backseat, in the Jeep Wagoneer's storage area. Grendel had prowled the small space restlessly for the first hundred miles before settling down on top of Alyson's leather suitcase.

"Grendel is ugly as sin," Sid continued, "and looks about that mean. Which works out fine, because he doesn't have much trouble scaring off the bad guys." He met Lenny's eyes in the rearview mirror. "He scare you?"

" 'Course not," Lenny said, his voice offended.

Sid nodded. "That's because you're smart

enough to see what's under his ugly hide. You know something? When somebody sees Grendel for the first time, I always, just for a couple of seconds, see him like they're seeing him. I just see what's on the outside, and it always surprises me. That's probably what happened to you with San León. You know this town. You know the good that's here. But just for a couple of seconds you saw it the way you figured we were seeing it."

Lenny didn't say anything. For a while there was only silence from the backseat, then he sat up straighter and said, "There's Saint Lucy's. Look . . . there's the church! Could we stop for a minute? I want to see if Father Mike is still there."

Sid pulled into the small gravel parking lot beside the church, and Lenny was out of the car before they had come to a full stop.

Alyson waited until Sid had stepped out of the car and had turned to follow Lenny before she touched his arm to gain his full attention.

"Wait." She cleared her throat. "I was wrong. I don't like admitting that. No, I *hate* admitting that. But the fact is, I was wrong, and you were right. You knew exactly what Lenny needed to hear. He didn't need the Pollyanna clichés I was about to hand him. He needed words that would guide him through hard reality. He isn't looking at the ugliness now. He's finding the good that's underneath."

His lips stretched in a wicked smile. "That hurt, didn't it?"

She almost shrugged but caught herself in

time. "A little . . . okay, a lot," she admitted. "But facts are facts. I was wrong. You were right."

She turned to walk away, but this time he caught her arm. When she raised a questioning brow, he glanced away. Then, inhaling slowly, he met her eyes. "I don't like changing the rules in the middle of the game," he said. "It confuses my simple brain. Okay . . . okay," he said when she continued to stare at him. "Look, I'm sorry. Now are you satisfied?"

She tilted her head, puzzled by the unexpected apology. "I suppose I am. At least, I would be if I knew what you were apologizing for."

Reaching up, he smoothed one finger over her lips. "I hurt you. I didn't mean to. My head felt like it was caught between two bulldozers, and I wasn't thinking straight." He exhaled roughly. "That's just a stupid excuse. The truth is, when I don't know how to handle something, I get mad. I'm sorry I got mad, and I'm sorry you got in the way."

She studied his flushed face for a moment, then smiled. "Next time I'll duck."

He laughed and took her arm as they walked toward the church. "You do that."

The sanctuary was as small and bare as the town. But here there was the kind of atmosphere Alyson had imagined. And there was charm. The sun's rays streaming through stained-glass windows filled every corner of the white-walled sanctuary with amber and rose light.

Lenny ran up to meet them. "He's still here! Come and meet him."

Father Michael Litner was a short tightly-built

man with blond hair and a red beard. When they reached him, he was shaking his head, muttering to himself: "I can't believe it." He glanced up at them and shook his head again. "The last time I saw him, he was a little boy. Now, he's grown. Our Lenny is a young man."

After the introduction the priest said, "Lenny tells me you've come to do some camping?"

Before leaving Dallas they had agreed they would tell no one about their quest for the "Golden Madonna." It would be disastrous for Lenny—and for the town—if they announced their intentions . . . and failed.

Sid nodded in response to Father Mike's question. "And to let Lenny see his hometown again."

Father Mike touched Lenny's head. "We've missed him."

"You have a beautiful church." Alyson glanced around. "Lenny tells me there's some kind of legend . . . about a missing Madonna."

The priest's laugh was rueful. "San León's only claim to fame." He walked to a small alcove to the right of the chancel. "The Madonna isn't fiction. It really existed. I've looked through all the old records. It was given to the church by the only wealthy man who's ever lived in the area. He wasn't Catholic. He wasn't even a religious man, but he liked the way the church helped the people in San León."

"So what happened to the Madonna?" Sid asked.

"No one knows." Father Mike chuckled. "There are plenty of theories. It's one of the hot topics over at the Easy Way Café. Some theories are pretty outrageous. One of my favorites is that someone in town offended God and He sent an angel down to take the Madonna. The only thing anyone really knows is that it was here one day, and the next it was gone." He sighed. "I just wish people would forget about it and stop blaming their bad luck on the missing Madonna. It's become a crutch. It's tough to get some of them— the older, superstitious ones—to even make an effort to improve their lives. They believe the town is 'accursed' and that no human effort can change that. Luck and prosperity will only return with the Blessed Mother."

Sid frowned. "Was San León prosperous before the Madonna disappeared?"

Father Mike groaned. "You'll learn not to ask questions like that. At least not to the superstitious. They don't want to hear the facts. They don't want to know that the town has always been poor. But don't get me wrong. I pray just as hard as the others for the return of the Madonna. If it were here, back where it belongs, the excuses would disappear. The people would have to make the effort to change. They would have to walk into the twentieth century."

Ten minutes later, when they were all back in the Jeep, Lenny said suddenly, "I know we're going to find it. I'm going to find it and bring it back to Father Mike."

"Sure you are," Sid said. "We're going to get started on that right now. Let's go pick up the horses and trailer."

Alyson sat up straighter. "Horses? I don't remember discussing horses."

"What's the matter, Princess? Don't tell me you forgot to pack your jodhpurs."

She glared at him. "Why do we need horses? Didn't we rent a Jeep specifically so we could travel over rough terrain?"

Sid's fingers clenched on the steering wheel. "You're using that tone again," he muttered. "The Jeep's fine to get us to the mesa, but if you had asked Lenny, he would have told you that the only trail leading to the top, if the trail still exists, was about five feet wide. I don't think I want to try that in the Jeep."

She turned and stared out the window. She should have asked Lenny. Damn it, why did Sid always have to be right?

"You said the trail was five feet wide." Alyson glanced around at the broken land. They were surrounded by uplifts and mesas, arroyos and thrusting rock. "Lenny, are you sure this is the right place?"

The boy gave her a pitying look. "The Three Brothers are over there," he said, indicating three needle spires. "Over there, that's Rainbow Rock. And this is Tall Man Mesa."

"Okay, it's the right place," she conceded grudgingly.

When Lenny walked to the horse trailer to talk to Sid, Alyson leaned against the Jeep and shaded her eyes with one hand, studying the boulder-strewn trail.

"Why couldn't he have found the Madonna somewhere closer to sea level?" she muttered to

Grendel who was standing next to her. "You look as lost as I feel."

She reached down to pet the dog, but when a rumbling growl came from low in his throat, she jerked her hand back.

It was at that moment that her spirit of adventure gave up the ghost. She was trapped out here with a man who had her pegged as a latter-day Marie Antoinette and would probably make her eat beef jerky—there was something unnatural about food that grew after it got in your mouth—a boy who tolerated her only because he had no choice, and a dog who kept eyeing her jugular vein.

"Are you going to cry?"

When she heard Sid's voice, she didn't turn to look at him. She kept staring toward the top of the mesa. "I hate you," she said, her voice calm. "I thought I only detested you, but now I realize that it's definitely hatred."

He laughed, then shook his head. "Where'd you learn to do that? That pouty thing you do with your mouth. It's the sexiest thing I've seen lately. Did they teach you that at finishing school? Come on, do it again."

She pushed away from the Jeep and shoved her way past him. "Oh . . . go chew on some jerky," she muttered, but the words were lost in his laughter.

Alyson spent the next two hours in brain-numbing terror. The horse she rode was gentle, but even gentle animals had minds of their own. They had their own quirks, their own neuroses. How could she be sure this particular animal wouldn't decide to commit suicide with her on its back?

It didn't. Although her heart stopped a couple of times when the horse stumbled on the narrow trail, Alyson made it to the top with no permanent damage.

When she stood back on solid ground at last, the sun was just about to disappear behind the horizon. She took a deep breath and raised her head, staring at the enormous sky.

"I made it," she said wryly. "Blair, I hope you're satisfied."

After a moment she lowered her gaze to the landscape, and her mouth dropped open in amazement. The dying sun had spilled molten metal—gold and bronze and copper—on the world, making the cruel barren landscape come to life with spectacular beauty.

When she heard a movement beside her, she glanced at Sid. "I think I'm in love. It's wild and free, and it goes on forever. It's too hard and mean to support any kind of life, but it's . . . it's *magnificent.*"

He smiled. "It's something, all right. God's country. The last bastion of the legendary Texas wildness and freedom."

"This is why he did it," she murmured.

"Why who did what?"

"Blair. Lenny's father. This is why he went all over the world, taking terrible risks to get to impossible places. I sweated blood on that torture-chamber thing you two called a trail, but now—" she waved a hand at the rapidly changing tableau, "It doesn't matter what I had to do to get here. Getting here is all that counts."

He was silent for a moment. "You were close to Lenny's father?"

"I loved him," she said quietly. "There will never be another man like Blair."

"And Blair is why you're here?"

"I'm here because of Lenny, but— Oh, I don't know. I guess, in my mind, Lenny's all tied up with Blair."

She could feel him staring at her. "Time to unload," he said abruptly.

As she watched him walk away, she wondered what on earth she had done to annoy him this time.

Sid squatted next to the campfire, poking at it with a piece of kindling. On the other side of the fire, near a canvas lean-to Sid had erected in the unlikely chance of rain, Lenny was sprawled in his sleeping bag.

The boy was worn out. He had been quiet since leaving the church that morning, quiet but not calm. Smoldering excitement was evident in the taut lines of his young face; he had wanted to go out and begin the search for the Madonna immediately.

Sid turned back to the fire. It had died down, leaving a pile of glowing red coals. He had always found a campfire hypnotic. But not tonight. *She* was several yards away from the fire, leaning against a massive boulder. The moon, big and low behind her, looked like a stage moon. It spotlighted her, drawing attention to her slender figure. Standing there in the silver light, she looked unaware, even innocent. It was a good act. A damned good act. But Sid had lost his sucker license years ago. He knew about women like her.

He had been barely twenty when he had learned his lesson. He had met Laura at a club. He was a regular. She was there for a night of slumming. Sid was young enough to be flattered by her interest and couldn't understand why, out of all the men in the club, she had chosen him.

After that first night, Sid had met her several more times in the club. He had basked in her attention, letting her flirt with him, encouraging her to touch him.

From a position of age and experience, he looked down on the unsophisticated young man he had been then with a mixture of sympathy and contempt. The poor sucker had eaten up all the attention Laura paid him. And worse, he actually believed Laura liked him. Maybe even loved him. Even though they came from different worlds, he thought she respected him as a man, especially when she began taking him on brief trips into her world, introducing him to her friends, including him in their highbrow activities.

At the time he believed he was in love with her. Now he knew he had been in love with the *idea* of her. He was intrigued by the idea of getting back at all the Mrs. Bartletts in his past. The ones who had mocked his grandfather's backcountry speech. The ones who snickered behind their hands, making fun of his bargain-basement clothes. The ones who were horrified at the idea of that wild Sid Sweet touching them.

Now he knew why he had become involved with Laura. It had not been love: when she told him the truth of why she had chased him, it had put a dent in his pride that had taken him years to repair. He could still hear her voice, her words so carefully enunciated.

"Women are drawn to you, Sid. Especially my kind of woman. There is something intrinsically dangerous about you. You're like a forest fire raging out of control. But darling you can't have believed I was serious about someone like you. I simply wanted to see how close I could get to the flames without getting singed."

For a while, when the hatred was still strong in him, he was galled by the fact that he had never made love to her. In his anger he believed it would have been some kind of compensation, some kind of payback. But eventually he realized he had missed nothing. From the distance of experience, he could see that Laura had nothing to give. There was no warmth in her, no capacity to love. Sex with her would have sickened him.

Now, because of his involvement with urban renewal and similar projects, Sid still ran into women like Laura. Society types who always looked so indulged, so bored. There was usually one who would send out signals, but he wouldn't be suckered twice. He avoided that kind of woman and stubbornly ignored their signals.

And he had thought he was too smart to get caught again. That's what he got for thinking. All Alyson had to do was move, and he had a knee-jerk reaction. Everything about her—the silky skin, the subtle scent, the pouty sensual lips— was a lure, drawing his attention against his will.

It was false advertising. Every line of her body promised heaven, but women like her could deliver only hell.

Alyson pushed away from the boulder and walked back to the campfire, lowering herself to the ground beside Sid. She had decided it was time to do something about the tension between them. He had asked for a truce, he had even apologized for blowing up at her, but there was still an uneasiness, a watchfulness, in the air between them. It couldn't continue. For Lenny's sake they had to get along.

"I can't believe you got him to go to bed," she said quietly. "I thought we were going to have to tie him up to keep him from going out with a flashlight."

"He's a stubborn little beggar."

She laughed softly. "He's that, all right. Sometimes it's difficult for me to believe he's Blair's son. They're so different."

"Tell me about Blair," he said abruptly. "How old was he when he came to live with your family?"

"Eleven. He came right after I got out of the hospital. I guess I was five then." She glanced at him, seeing the question in his eyes. "I had polio." She smiled. "My parents were totally incensed. Polio was supposed to happen to other people, not to Wildes. In fact, I'm surprised they didn't sue every doctor in the state for allowing me to miss the vaccine. Sometimes I think they really believed I did it on purpose, just to be perverse. Anyway, I had to stay in bed for several years. Lord, how I hated that bed. And the *therapy* . . . it hurt like crazy." She paused. "Then Blair came. You know how kids, especially boys, are so contemptuous of anyone younger and weaker? Well, it wasn't that way with Blair. My parents wanted only to pamper and protect me. In other words, they tried to keep me away from life."

She stared up at the sky. "You can't imagine how lonely it was," she said softly. "But Blair saved me. Physically, I was an invalid, but he refused to let me turn into an emotional invalid as well. He visited me every day after school, and he made those times exciting. He would spin stories for me, fantastic adventures. But he wouldn't let me just listen. He made me join in." She turned toward him as the memory captured her. "Together we went out to explore the world without ever leaving my bedroom. He subscribed to *National Geographic,* so there was always somewhere new to go, something new and exciting to see.

"It was wonderful," she said with a small sigh. "But I guess I should have known nothing that wonderful can last forever. One day, when I was eleven, he simply wasn't there. He was only seventeen, but he was gone. Out on his own in the world. When he didn't come to my room, my parents— Mother and Daddy were angry, I could see it in their faces, but they wouldn't tell me what had happened. They just said he wouldn't be living with us anymore."

"He didn't even leave me a note." When she glanced at Sid, her smile was self-mocking. "I was sick for a week. But then, about three months after he left, the first package arrived in the mail. Mrs. Teasey—she's our housekeeper—saved it for me. She loved Blair too, so she didn't say anything to my parents because she was afraid they wouldn't let me keep it."

She smiled. "It was a little Mexican doll. I still have it on the table beside my bed. The packages came periodically for the next few years, and every time I received one, I would make up stories about the gifts, stories about where he was and what he had been doing when he found them. I would pretend that I had been there too. It was almost like having Blair with me again."

She shifted her position restlessly. "Then suddenly the gifts stopped coming. Although I didn't understand it at the time, that must have been when he married Sandra. By then I was older and more physically fit. His neglect hurt, but it didn't make me sick," she said with a smile. "I started going out and buying things for myself. I would pick out anything that struck my fancy, anything absurd or exotic, and pretend it came from Blair. I bought the kind of thing he would have sent if he could. You see, that kept the ties between us intact. The gifts and the fantasies."

"Fantasies?"

"Sad, isn't it?" She smiled wryly. "My reality

never measured up to Blair's. He was out doing exciting things, and I wanted desperately to be doing those things as well, but I was too much of a coward. Except in my dreams."

She drew her knees up and leaned her chin against them. "No one in my life has ever measured up to Blair. No one could."

For a few moments the only sounds were the soft pops from the dying fire. Then Sid said, "Do you know what your cousin did when he stopped playing Errol Flynn and settled down?"

There was something about his tone that made her skin prickle with irritation. "What do mean, what did he do?"

"I mean did he sit around thinking brilliant thoughts? Did he join the exciting world of professional truck driving? What did he do? Didn't Lenny ever tell you?"

For some reason the question made her uncomfortable. Uncomfortable and defensive and resentful. "Blair was an inspired artist, even as a teenager. I always assumed— The subject never came up," she finished shortly.

"Well I asked." His voice was suddenly angry. "The good Saint Blair couldn't hold down a job. According to Len, his father never stayed at any job for longer than six months. He would get himself fired, or he would quit. When the money ran out, when they were down to their last box of saltines, he would go out and find another job." He paused to study her stiff features. "Not a real secure environment for a kid."

"Did Lenny complain?" she asked tightly. "Does

he resent the fact that his father didn't have a steady job?"

He gave a short bark of laughter. "You've got to be kidding. Len's as bad as you. He carries this invisible shrine around with him all the time. In his eyes his father could do no wrong. He makes all kinds of excuses. But like your fantasies, they're all lies. And I'll tell you what. Unless you do something about it, the kid is going to grow up thinking that's the way a real man does it. Your job is to teach him that a man lives up to his responsibilities. You've got to let him know that being a jerk, like his father, is not a worthwhile goal."

"*Shut up*." The words were quiet and intense. "Don't you *dare* talk about Blair like that. You don't know anything. You can't even conceive of the kind of man he was. Keeping a job wasn't the most important thing. The most important thing was the way he loved his son. Lenny will always have that to fall back on. No matter what happens in the future, he can remember that his father loved him."

"Yeah," he said in a sarcastic drawl. "He loved him all right. He loved the kid so much, he left him in the care of a vicious bitch who terrorized him any damn time she felt like it."

The next instant she moved to slap him. But before she could, her wrist was held in a vise-like grip.

"I told you once I'm no gentleman," he growled. "Hit me, and I'll hit back." He paused, studying her face. "The truth isn't pretty, but you're going to hear it just this once. Every time Sandra felt like going out for a little fun, she locked the kid in the closet. And you know what his father did about it? He would talk to her and get her to promise not to do it again. A man of action, your cousin. Sandra would keep the promise for a while. Until the next time she got the urge to leave. Then she'd shove Len in the closet again."

He turned away from what he saw in her face. "That's the truth about your precious Blair."

Wrapping her arms around her body, Alyson began to rock back and forth. "It wasn't that way," she whispered hoarsely. "It couldn't have been that way. You didn't know him. He was so loving. So gentle. You— You're different. A man like you could never understand someone like Blair."

When she placed her hands on the ground, preparing to rise to her feet, his fingers closed around her forearm and jerked her back so that she fell hard against him.

"Let me go," she spat at him. "Just keep your hands off me!"

He smiled, and it was the most terrifying thing she had ever seen. "Afraid of getting dirty?"

"*Let go.*"

She leaned away from him, but he reached out and grasped her chin, holding her tightly so that his fingers dug into her cheeks, hurting her.

"One of these days, lady," he said in a rough whisper, then brushed a kiss, hard and brief, across her lips. "One of these days."

When he abruptly let her go, she was shaking so hard that she stumbled when she rose to her feet. He made no attempt to help her, and he didn't speak again. But she could feel his gaze on her long after she had crawled into the sleeping bag near Lenny.

Six

First thing the next morning the three of them, four including Grendel, rode out to look over the area. Alyson avoided looking at Sid, concentrating on the scenery. It was safer that way.

The top of the mesa looked remarkably like the flat below, and there wasn't a lot of vegetation, mostly desert plants—yuccas, sotols, agaves, and the ever-present prickly pear. There wasn't even much dirt. The surface was covered by smooth cream-colored rock with patches of rough grass growing through the cracks—a severe landscape dominated by an outsize sky. The white glare from the sun, the silver waves of heat rising from the rocks, added to the feeling of isolation.

Alyson pulled out her handkerchief, pushed back her hat, and wiped her gritty, perspiring forehead. The day before, they had arrived at their campsite at sundown, and she hadn't realized it would be so hot.

I will not be the first one to complain, she told herself stubbornly. Sid and Lenny had to be feeling the heat as much she did, even though neither seemed to be melting, which she definitely was. She was positive her arms were thinner than they had been the day before.

She glanced at Sid's back, then away again. Last night and again today she had tried to think about what he had told her. She wasn't so naive as to believe that he had lied. Lenny had given her enough hints. She had simply failed to pick up on them. Maybe she hadn't wanted to. Maybe she'd even suspected all along. But now the truth was out, and her shock and disillusionment had been relegated to second place.

Something was getting in the way. Or someone. Every time she remembered the look in Sid's eyes when he had held her chin and kissed her the night before, the memory took up her whole mind and all her emotion.

"What do you think, Len?" Sid, whose horse was in the lead, turned in the saddle to ask the question.

Surprisingly Lenny didn't shrug. He just kept looking around, his expression confused and upset. "I don't know. There were some tall cactuses. I remember more tall cactus." His voice held a note of panic as he shook his head and gripped the reins tighter. "I can't remember any of this stuff."

Alyson moved her horse up beside his, taking care to stay out of Grendel's way. "Don't worry about it. Let's just keep wandering around. You'll see. It won't be long before you'll see something familiar. All you have to do right now is recognize one gully, one rock. That will give us a place to start."

"Aly's right," Sid said. "Just scope the place out. Don't try for any big stuff right now, like where the hole in the ground is. Just start small, and the rest will come back to you. There's no need to rush it. We've got plenty of time."

As he spoke, their eyes met across Lenny, and it made her angry that she was the first to look away. Apparently it didn't have the same effect on Sid. His mood was noticeably lighter as they once again picked up the slow pace. He and Lenny began cutting up, challenging each other in interchanges that were thoroughly male, therefore excluding. She was glad to see Lenny in a better mood, but that didn't stop her from resenting Sid.

A little over half an hour later Sid drew back on the reins, pulling his horse to a halt. He glanced at her, then at Lenny. "It's getting hotter."

"No doubt." Lenny's drawling sarcasm transformed the latter word into something that sounded like "duh."

Sid grinned. "Why don't we go back to camp for a while? We could sit under the lean-to and eat lunch, maybe rest a little while. We can try again when it cools off."

Say yes, Lenny, she begged silently. Please, say yes.

She wanted to speak up, but she didn't want to be the one to disappoint her cousin. Okay . . . okay, she admitted to herself. It wasn't only

Lenny. She didn't want to give Sid the satisfaction of seeing her fold.

She smiled at the boy. "I don't need a break," she lied. "Do you need a break, Lenny?"

"Not me."

She glanced at Sid. "Oh, I'm sorry, Sid. I forgot you were older. If you need to rest, of course we'll go back."

Lenny giggled, saying, "Good one, Aly."

"I'll probably hold up a little while longer," Sid said. "You take the lead, Len."

He moved his horse aside to allow Lenny to pass him, and all the while he kept his gleaming brown eyes on her. When they began moving again, he slowed his pace so that she eventually drew even with him.

"Good one, Aly," he murmured.

"I know, I know," she said. " 'One of these days, lady.' "

Chuckling, he jerked on the reins, turning his horse aside to let her pass.

Not more than fifteen minutes had passed before Lenny circled around to talk to Sid. "I don't want to stop or anything, except that thing you said about lunch sounds okay. But we don't have to go back to camp," he said quickly. "I could ride back and get some food for lunch. Then we could eat out here."

"In the boiling heat," Alyson muttered under her breath. "Sounds like a treat to me."

Sid glanced around. "Okay, we'll do that. Me and Aly will wait in the shade of that rock while you play chef."

Alyson looked at the rock. There wasn't enough

shade there to cover a large bug. Like a scorpion. *Don't think about the scorpions. Or the snakes.*

"Sounds good to me," she said, but somehow her voice was just a shade less bright than she had intended.

After Lenny rode away, taking Grendel along for company, Sid led the way to the small overhang. Alyson slid stiffly from the saddle, gripping the saddle horn when her legs went wobbly for a moment.

"What's the matter, doesn't your pampered little butt fit a Western saddle?"

She looked at him over her shoulder. She was too tired to snarl, so she simply raised her chin. "My 'pampered little butt' fits just fine, thank you. I'm just waiting until the ground stops trembling. Oh, shut up," she muttered as she slumped down in the shade to the sound of his laughter. "I haven't ridden in three years. The necessary muscles are hibernating or something."

She took off her hat and patted her face and neck with the already damp handkerchief. As she pulled the yellow cotton shirt away from her skin, she wished she had enough nerve to reach inside and wipe away the perspiration that was trickling beneath her breasts.

Sid didn't sit. He stood leaning against the rock, his hat pushed back on his head. Alyson had wondered at their first meeting where he fit. Now she knew. His clothes—the tight faded jeans, the open-neck plaid shirt, the stained Western hat, and worn boots—should have made him look like an urban cowboy, but they didn't. Not at all.

He looked like the genuine article. He looked as if he belonged.

Shifting her position to get away from the sharp rock under her hip, she said, "Lenny's getting desperate."

He nodded. "He needs to relax for a couple of hours. He's been checking out every inch of ground we pass. If he keeps straining his brain like that, it's going to explode."

"I'm worried about him," she admitted. "I still believe finding the Madonna would help get him on the right track, but I have to admit I didn't think about what would happen if he doesn't find it. I didn't think about how failure would affect him."

"He won't fail," he said quietly. "Len will find it. He'll find it if I have to blow up the whole damned mesa."

She studied the intensity in his strong face. "Why is it so important to you? I know you care about him and want him to succeed, but it's more than that, isn't it?"

He didn't answer immediately. He stood staring at the blue-white sky awhile, then he said, "Len doesn't think much of himself right now. I want that to change. That way, someday when somebody tells him he's worthless, he won't believe it. He won't automatically accept someone else's estimation of his value."

She tilted her head so she could see him better. "Did someone . . . Did that happen to you? Did someone tell you you're worthless?"

He smiled. " 'Someone'? I've been told that, maybe not in those exact words but near enough, more times than I can count. It took me a long time for me to believe that they were wrong." He frowned and shifted his position, then shook his head restlessly. "Anyway, I don't want it to be that way for Len. When I was a kid, I thought nice clothes and a fancy house would have done it for me. I thought if I had that stuff, it would make me anybody's equal. Because of you, Len's got the clothes and the house, and that's good. Because no matter what anybody says, money and the things it can buy will make a difference in how other kids, his first judges, treat him. But there's got to be more than that. Something that nobody can buy for him. Something that comes from inside a person. A gut-deep thing. It's this confidence, this quiet assurance that doesn't need to go around blowing its own horn. It's just there, and because it's there, you don't have to fight the people who put you down. Knowing the truth is enough."

Alyson stared at him in silence. It was the most he had said since she'd met him, in word count and in content. The intense speech gave her insights she wasn't sure she was ready to handle. Moments later she glanced up and found him watching her.

"How come you're not still mad?" he asked abruptly. "I did a pretty good job of busting your pretty bubble last night. How come you're not still spitting at me?"

She didn't say anything. Avoiding his eyes, she wiped her throat again with the handkerchief.

"You haven't admitted it yet." The words were

an incredulous accusation. "You're still hiding from the truth. Judas priest, what a coward."

His contemptuous tone brought her chin up. "I don't owe you an explanation. I don't have to make excuses to you for what I think and feel." When the silence drew out, she clenched her fists and said, "Okay, I tried to think about it. I really tried, but— The thing is, for almost my whole life Blair has been . . . he's been a symbol. He was the banner I held up in my mind. Not a single thing happened to me that I didn't ask myself what Blair would think about it, what Blair would do in the same situation. He was the yardstick against which I measured every man who came into my life. It may sound a little obsessive, but I can't help that. That's the way it was. And now you're telling me the man who has played such an important part in my life didn't even exist. That's challenging a basic belief. It's like telling me truth is an illusion. It's like telling me I've based my life on a lie." She pushed several loose strands of hair from her sticky forehead. "I need some time to acclimatize. Losing the . . . *essence* of Blair has left a gaping hole. I'm going to have to recast my life, my whole way of thinking."

He drew his head back, and his eyes were narrow as he stared at her. "Lady, that's not a little obsessive, that's sick. You're telling me if a man didn't measure up to your cousin, you dumped him? Since I know you put Len's father right up there with the angel Gabriel, there couldn't have been many men who were allowed to snuggle up to you."

He paused, still studying her flushed face. "Wait

a minute . . . oh, no, that's too much. You're not trying to tell me—"

"I'm not trying to tell you anything," she said stiffly. "You seem to be carrying the conversation just fine, all on your own."

"There haven't been *any* men," he said, shaking his head in disbelief. "All this time you've been sitting around waiting for a man who's a combination of Indiana Jones, Tom Cruise, and Bishop Desmond Tutu. You're a piece of work, you know that? You're really something."

"Actually," she said, her voice carefully cool, "my personal life is none of your business. I refuse to apologize for not having a list of men to my credit." She inhaled deeply, her nostrils flaring with anger. "With my mind, if not my heart, I thank you for giving me the facts about Blair. I needed to know for Lenny."

"Yeah, you sound real tickled about it."

She clenched her fists. "For Lenny, I'm glad I have the truth. For myself, I resent the hell out of it. Yes, I'm a coward. I resent having to face the future without even the memory of a man who meant a lot to me. But most of all I resent—"

She broke off when she felt drops of cool moisture on her face. "What *is* that?"

"I believe they call it rain," he said dryly.

She scrambled to her feet. "Rain?"

Staring up at the sky, she spotted a thin line of clouds and eagerly moved from the rock, raising her face to the drops that fell harder and harder, cooling her skin, drenching her hair and clothes.

"It's wonderful!" she shouted, twirling around.

He caught her arm. "Finish what you were saying. Most of all you resent . . . what?"

"It's not important. I can't hold on to resentment in the middle of a miracle. It's *raining*."

He grinned. "Miracle? Oh, I see what you mean. God looked down here and saw that the crème de la crème of all His creations was hot and said, 'We can't have this,' so He sent a shower to cool little Aly off."

"It could happen," she said, laughing as she licked the moisture from her lips.

He went suddenly still, keeping his gaze trained on her face as he reached out to smooth the damp curls from her cheek. For long moments their eyes held, and something powerful and compelling passed between them.

Then, seconds later, he shifted his gaze away from her and cleared his throat. "Playtime is over," he said roughly. "I want you to tell me what you were going to say. Or should I tell you? Most of all you resent the fact that I was the one to tell you the truth about your wonderful Blair." His fingers tightened on her arm. "Isn't that what you were going to say?"

She let out a harsh breath. "Why can't you just let it go? For heaven's sake, you can even spoil a miracle." Her features tightened in resentment. "*Yes*. That's exactly what I was going to say. Satisfied now? I resented hearing it from you because you mock everything. I resent it because you *loved* smashing my illusions. You did it cruelly and deliberately."

He twisted her arm behind her, bringing her

body in close contact with his. "You got that right. Because they damned well needed smashing," he said, his voice low and intense. "I didn't know how much until a few minutes ago. You've been saving yourself, waiting for a hero, and guess what, lady? It ain't gonna happen. You're frigid, you don't want what a *real* man could give you. You would rather have something perfect—something cold, dead, and perfect—than something imperfect but warm and alive. Something rough . . . and hot," he whispered hoarsely.

Jerking her arm loose, she backed away from him and wiped the rain from her eyes. "You have no right to pass judgment," she said, her voice sharp with anger. "But if you want to talk about warped, what about what you're doing right now? And don't pretend you don't know what you're doing. Since the minute we met, you've been making those not-so-subtle sexual threats. Why? I'm no danger to you. You do it to keep some kind of wall between us. You don't even want me. You're simply trying to scare me off . . . because you're afraid if I get too close, I'll see something you don't want me to see. That's it, isn't it? *Isn't it?*"

"*Shut up!*" he rasped out, taking a step forward. "You don't know what the hell you're talking about."

"Don't I?"

She had said the words belligerently, but the belligerence was false. The truth was, she was suddenly overwhelmingly frightened, which wasn't surprising, considering the look on his face. What was surprising was that she was not frightened by him, nor by what he might do to her. It was something in *her* that made her afraid. Some emotion that seemed to be building to the point of explosion.

Swinging away from him, she began to run. The wet rock was treacherously slick, and she had gone only a short distance when she slipped and fell to her knees. She glanced over her shoulder. Through the falling rain she saw him. He was still following. As she watched, he ran into a rusty length of barbed wire that had become entangled in a creosote bush. It didn't even slow him down. He simply ripped it loose, leaving a long tear in the denim that covered one muscular thigh.

With both hands she wiped the rain from her face, then scrambled to her feet and began to run again. She still wasn't sure what she was running from or why. She only knew she had to get away before something happened, something unexpected and irreversible.

When she reached a rocky rise, Alyson didn't pause. She searched for a foothold and began to climb. In almost the same instant she felt his hands on her, swinging her around. But still she refused to give up. She fought him with a desperation that was as incomprehensible as it was real. She knocked his hat from his head and heard him grunt when her foot connected with his shin.

Inevitably, her struggles unbalanced them, and they fell heavily to the wet rock. Moving quickly, he pinned her arms down, sliding one knee across both her legs as he swore under his breath.

When she finally stopped fighting, his body was pressed heavily against hers, and there was only the combined sound of their harsh labored breathing.

"You said I only wanted to scare you," he said after a moment. "Is it working?"

"Yes," she whispered hoarsely. "I'm scared. Will you let me up now?"

He didn't answer. He just kept staring down at her. But he was no longer staring at her face. Glancing down, she saw that the rain had fused her thin cotton blouse and the silk bra to her skin, making them virtually transparent.

Slowly raising his gaze, he met her eyes. "You said a lot of stupid things back there. The most stupid was that I don't really want you. I want you." His voice was harsh and uneven. "If you knew how much I want you, it would blow your closed little mind."

Before he finished the last word, his head descended, and his mouth pressed against hers with bruising force. The hard force of his lips shocked her body into instant, profound awareness, and as though he recognized her response, almost immediately the quality of the kiss changed. It was no less forceful, but the anger was gone.

Pulling her arms free, she threw them around his neck. And there in the middle of a desert rainstorm, they became immersed in each other, eating each other up. It was as though their mutual need had been building for a lifetime of cold, lonely years. As though each had been deprived of something fundamental, something indispensably precious, and they were now trying to make up for the deficiency.

With brusque, urgent movements he pulled her blouse loose from her jeans, pushing it up to unhook the front closure on her bra. When she felt the rain on her bare skin, it became a part of the intolerable ecstasy. He gathered both her breasts in the palms of his hands and squeezed them together, pressing groaning kisses to the voluptuous flesh than began sucking and licking the dampness from her.

Need, more critical than anything she had felt before, demanded she do something, anything, to get closer to him and the sensations he had created especially for her. With shaking fingers she unbuttoned his wet shirt and slid her hands inside, reveling in the damp warmth, the hard rough texture of his chest.

"You feel so good," she said in a ragged whisper. "You feel *so damn good*."

Raising his head from her breasts, he captured the words with a hungry kiss. Instinctively she parted her lips to accept his tongue, eager for it, dying for it. Their bodies moved together rhythmically, her slick breasts sliding against his wet rough chest, her hips grinding into his.

"Dear sweet heaven," he rasped out.

He sounded in pain, as though he could barely force the words out, and she knew exactly how he felt. There was pain. Sweet primal pain. There was torment that couldn't be separated from the volcanic joy.

Moving her hands impulsively to the wet denim covering his buttocks, she dug her fingers into the hard muscle, urging him closer. In response he groaned his pleasure into her mouth and shifted slightly away from her. His fingers were tugging at the snap of her jeans when they heard Grendel barking in the distance.

His face swam before her eyes, and she blinked away the vertigo, staring at him as he stared at her. His pupils were dilated, his features looking as stunned as she felt. For long tense moments they simply stared at each other. Then, as though realization struck simultaneously, he averted his gaze and she blushed.

He pushed away from her slowly, his movements awkward as he allowed her the freedom to sit up. Her fingers shook uncontrollably as she fastened her bra and pulled her blouse down to cover her breasts. Glancing at him from the corners of her eyes, she saw him shove both hands through his wet hair.

"Okay, so maybe I was wrong too," he said, his voice hoarse. "You're not frigid."

She moaned and scooted back to lean against the boulder behind her, closing her eyes as she tried to swallow the lump of humiliation that was caught in her throat.

By the time Lenny reached them, the rain was gone. The thin line of clouds had passed, and the sun was busy evaporating any remaining moisture. Everything was back to normal. Almost.

Seven

Something had changed between them, Alyson decided as she sat again in the meager shade of the rock.

She waited two beats, then almost laughed aloud. Minutes earlier she had been rolling around half naked in the rain with a man who detested her, one touch from him having loosed all the emotions she had kept buried for a lifetime, and now she had decided that *something* had changed between them? That had to be the understatement of the year. Something hadn't changed. Everything had changed.

They had been aware of each other from the very beginning, but never so acutely as now. Every look, every accidental touch, was emphasized, magnified in importance. There had always been tension between them, but in the past the tension was antagonistic, two magnets stubbornly, repeatedly repelling. Now the tension was devastatingly sensual, and the same two magnets were drawing relentlessly, inexorably closer.

"That rain was really excellent," Lenny said through a mouthful of food.

"Excellent," Alyson agreed, giving him a small twitching smile. "Pass me the canteen. You make the world's best sandwiches, but for some reason, my tongue keeps sticking to the roof of my mouth."

For lunch Lenny had brought them sandwiches containing a smear of grape jelly and approximately an inch of peanut butter per sandwich. Taking the canteen from him, Alyson carefully wiped the lip, then closed one eye and peered into the dark interior.

"There had better not be any crumbs in here," she murmured before taking a drink of the lukewarm water.

She was moving to replace the cap when, without a word, Sid reached over and took the canteen from her. He turned it up and drank deeply, the muscles in his throat moving rhythmically as he kept his eyes trained on her face. After a moment he lowered the container and, still watching her, slowly wiped his mouth with the back of his hand.

Alyson couldn't move. His gaze pushed her against the rock, pinning her there with unforgivable ease. All he had to do was look at her, a simple little glance, and she felt everything she had felt when he kissed her. Everything she had felt when he touched her naked flesh. Everything she had felt when she hungrily explored his body.

Abruptly he broke eye contact, releasing her, and she almost whimpered in relief and regret.

Sid put the cap back on the canteen and laid it aside. He couldn't let himself look into her gray eyes again. It was almost like making love to her. Glancing at her from the corners of his eyes, he studied the pure sleek lines of her face. She looked unchanged. She looked serene, at peace with the world. Damn her to hell, she looked as though nothing had happened. She didn't seem to feel what he felt, as if she had just stepped over the edge of the world, free-falling into the unknown.

In the few seconds he had held her, her warm bare breasts pressed against him, Sid's range of possibilities had exploded. The way he felt when she reached out to touch him should have been beyond the scope of ordinary man. She had made him feel like an unskilled laborer, like an inexperienced kid. And the crazy part was, he *was* inexperienced. He had made love to a lot of women, but never—not once—had he felt anything like what he felt when he kissed her. How could he have ever imagined he would feel something like that?

Even now, just thinking about it, he found himself sliding back into the feeling, recalling it with a mixture of wonder and fear. But even as the sensation took hold, he shook free of it. He couldn't let it happen. It was obvious she hadn't felt the same thing. And even if she had, he couldn't lose sight of reality. It would be stupid to get involved with a woman like her. He had played that game once, and he had learned his lesson. Women like Alyson Wilde weren't for the likes of Sid Sweet.

For a long time Alyson kept her eyes closed, praying for the normal world, the world she had gladly abandoned while she was in Sid's arms, to return.

Seconds later Lenny belched; her prayer answered in a crude way.

When she opened one eye to look at him, he shrugged. "It snuck up on me," he explained. "Peanut butter's got a real kick, doesn't it?"

Sid cuffed him on the back of the head. "Disgusting little twit." He rose to his feet. "You people ready to go fight some more windmills?"

"What windmills?" Lenny asked, scrambling up. "There ain't one single windmill in a hundred miles."

"Lenny," she said, watching him follow Sid toward the horses. *"Lenny!"*

He stopped and turned around, throwing her a questioning glance. "Yeah?"

She stood up and moved closer to the boy. "There are a lot of things I will ignore. There are a lot of things I will let slide. 'Ain't' is not one of them," she said firmly. "It's pure laziness. There are legitimate casual words you can use instead. I wouldn't even mind if you used 'idn't' in place of 'isn't'. But *not* 'ain't.' "

"Loosen up, Aly," Sid called over his shoulder. "We're in a different part of the world now. Different country, different language. Who knows, before we get through, you may be throwing around a few 'ain'ts' yourself."

"I would rather eat dirt," she said, the words slow, concise, and distinctly prim.

Lenny and Sid laughed, and as the latter swung into the saddle, his gaze met hers. "You could be doing some of that too."

It took them almost two hours to reach the northern edge of the mesa. Several times, as they rode slowly across the barren land, Lenny thought he caught a glimpse of something—a break in the rock surface, a slight difference in the distant view—that looked familiar to him, but each time it turned out to be a false alarm.

When Sid signaled it was time for a break, Alyson sighed in relief. She slid from the saddle, still grasping the saddle horn, and turned to watched Lenny walk over to the edge of the mesa.

"He's tensing up again."

She blinked several times in startled reaction. She hadn't heard Sid's approach. Moistening her lips, she threw him a glance and said, "Do you think it would help if I go talk to him?"

He shook his head. "It would be better if he did the talking, but Len's not the most communicative guy I've ever met." He studied the brooding boy for a moment. "Maybe something more physical would work. I'll see what I can do to take his mind off things," he said as he moved away from her.

From where she stood, Alyson couldn't hear what he said to Lenny, but a few minutes later the two of them walked back to Sid's horse, and Sid pulled a rifle from the saddle holster.

She glanced from Sid to Lenny, then from Lenny to Sid. "Lenny annoys me sometimes, too," she said slowly, "but don't you think shooting him is a little drastic?"

Lenny gave a loud snort of laughter. "He's not going to shoot me. He's going to teach me how to use the rifle. See, he ain't—"

"Give me the gun," she said the second the word left Lenny's lips.

Lenny ducked behind Sid. "I meant 'isn't.' "

"Sure you did." She raised her head and met Sid's eyes. "You're going to teach him to shoot? The very thought makes me nervous. *Guns* make me nervous. And the idea of letting Lenny shoot one is shocking, not to mention a bit injudicious. It would be like handing an Uzi to an angry gorilla." She shook her head. "Somehow it doesn't seem quite civilized."

"I hate to disillusion you," Sid said, smiling slightly, "but we don't live in a civilized world. It would be real nice if guns didn't exist. Real nice. But they do. That's reality. The suckers are everywhere, city and country, and as long as they are, Len needs to know how to handle one. He needs to be taught how to keep from hurting himself or anyone else when he comes in contact with a gun. Which he will, sooner or later. You can make book on it."

He raised one heavy brow at her still-doubtful expression. "Knowledge never hurt anybody. I figured you'd be the first to agree with that."

"I do. But . . . okay, you're right," she said,

reluctantly admitting the validity of his argument. "As long as they exist, he needs to know."

"Y'all finished?" Lenny asked, his tone impatient. "Can I go blow something away now?"

When Sid cuffed him on the back of the head, he yelped and reached back to rub the spot. "Can't that cause brain damage or something? Hey, Aly, isn't that, like, child abuse?"

She cuffed him on the back of the head. "With you, my darling, it's, like, necessary." She touched his arm. "Watch what you're doing, okay?"

His muttered "whatever" was all the reassurance he would allow her.

She stood and watched from a safe distance. At first she was nail-bitingly nervous, but gradually she realized that Sid knew what he was doing. He took time to explain everything to Lenny in detail. She had a qualm or two when, instead of giving the boy a list of rules on gun safety, Sid told him graphic, sometimes gruesome stories of friends and acquaintances who hadn't followed the rules. But she kept her mouth firmly shut.

As she had stood watching them, an outlandish notion had taken hold, surprising her. What was going on between Lenny and Sid was man stuff, and she would be out of her league if she tried to interfere. Nice thoughts, idealistic concepts, wouldn't make a dent in Lenny's stubborn little brain, but hard reality would. And as strange as it seemed, she trusted Sid to do what was right where Lenny was concerned. He seemed to be trying to equip the boy to face the world—hard, cold place that it was.

"Aly!"

She pushed away from the sheltering boulder when she heard Lenny's voice. Until this trip, no one had ever called her Aly. In fact, she had never had a nickname of any kind. Smiling, she decided it had a nice ring to it.

'Sorry," she called out. "My mind was wandering. Did you blow away something interesting?"

"I hit the rock twice."

There was distinct pride in his voice, and the sound brought an unexpected lump to her throat.

"Watch me," he yelled before turning back to Sid.

Lenny missed the rock on the next two tries, but after his coach gave him additional instructions, he hit it three times in a row.

Alyson applauded enthusiastically. "I'll have to start calling you Wild Bill."

He ran over to her. "I've gotta get me a rifle. Can I, Aly?" he asked, dancing around her in excitement. "You saw how good I am. Can I have a rifle of my own?"

"Oh, Lenny. I don't know." She glanced at the man walking toward them. Her newfound trust had just taken a nosedive. "A gun, Lenny?"

"Slow down, idiot," Sid said when he reached them. "You're too young and too dumb to have your own rifle."

The insults didn't even faze Lenny. "I'm not that young," he argued.

Sid laughed. "I'm glad you didn't dispute the dumb part. I tell you what. We'll start going to target practice a couple of hours a week. And in your spare time, you read up and learn how to take care of a gun. Maybe take a couple of safety classes. If you stick it out, and when you prove to both Aly and me that you know what you're doing, then we'll talk about getting you a rifle of your own."

Lenny let out a war whoop, slapped Sid's hand in exultant gratitude, then ran to gather up the spent cartridges to keep as souvenirs.

When Alyson slowly turned to look at Sid, he grinned. "Wait, don't hit me yet," he said hastily. "I have a plan."

"There's good news," she muttered. "Correct me if I'm wrong, but wasn't it one of your little 'plans' that got this gun fever started in the first place? I'll tell you right now, Sid, I will *not* have a gun in my house. Not now, not ever. And especially not in the hands of a maniacal thirteen-year-old hit man."

By the time she had finished her speech, he was shaking with laughter. "Relax," he said. "It won't go that far. Trust me on this one. Right now Len is picturing himself in the role of a Western Rambo, but by the time I get through with him, he won't find any glamour in guns. He'll know them inside out, upside down, and backwards. And he'll get bored with the whole thing. That way, no one will ever be able to tempt him with the forbidden excitement of firearms. He'll know all about guns, and they'll hold no mysteries for him."

She remained silent for a moment, absorbing what he had said. "Okay, I'll accept that," she said finally. "Just keep in mind that I'll be watching. And the second your plan starts to go awry, we'll switch to my plan instead."

"What's your plan?"

"Shave his head and send him to a monastery."

Grinning in appreciation, he shook his head. "It won't be necessary. Not that I wouldn't give a nickel to see Len turned loose on a bunch of unsuspecting monks," he added.

She laughed and leaned against the rock, feeling completely comfortable with him, but seconds later their eyes met, and instantly the laughter faded. Without a sound or movement to warn her, the atmosphere between them became charged. Awareness, hotter and more intense than the desert heat, surrounded them, binding them together. A physical flashback to the scene in the rain. Alyson couldn't speak. She could only stand and stare at him, her heart pounding as she shook her head in a barely perceptible movement.

A stunned look darkened his brown eyes as he reached out to her. She could have sworn he wasn't in control of his own movements as he touched her, brushing his fingertips across one rigid nipple.

It was her sharp intake of breath that finally broke the spell. Sid blinked twice, swore under his breath, then turned and walked away.

Alyson's knees buckled, and she sat down abruptly, whispering "*Oh, no*" over and over again.

She wanted to go somewhere private so she could sort out the emotions that were suddenly running wild within her. She wanted that badly.

But if she had learned one thing since Lenny had come to her, it was that when you have a child, you can't fall apart when you feel like it. Someone, somewhere, at some point in the distant past had made up an immutable rule: If you're going to accept responsibility for a child, you have to act like an adult. As far as she was concerned, the rule stank.

Taking a deep breath, she clenched her fists and stood up, walking slowly to join Sid and Lenny. Surprisingly she put on a pretty good act for the next few minutes. She even managed to laugh when Lenny suggested he teach her to shoot.

"Why not?" he persisted. "It's easy. Give me a coupla minutes, and I'll teach you everything I know."

She shook her head. "If I ever lose my grip on sanity, if I ever should reach the point of having so little judgment that I actually want to learn how to handle a gun, you can be reasonably sure I won't go to someone whose expertise can be transferred in a 'coupla minutes.' "

He glanced at Sid. "What'd she say?"

"I think she said she'll let you teach her when hell freezes over." Sid glanced at her, briefly meeting her eyes. "Len has a point though. You need to learn. No, wait, just listen for a minute. We talked about how important it was for Len to have firsthand knowledge. Well, the same goes for you. How can you make any decisions in the future unless you know what you're talking about? Are you going to take Len's word that he knows what he's doing?"

"I hate it when you're right," she grumbled. "I really hate it. Okay, I'll learn, but do I have to do it now? I don't know about you people, but I'm tired and gritty and hungry. I want to go back to camp and luxuriate in a tepid sponge bath before sampling the dubious culinary delights in store for us tonight."

Lenny and Sid glanced at each other, then Sid shrugged his shoulders. "You got me," he said. "She lost me right after 'tired and gritty.' "

"Let's go home," she moaned.

The ride back to camp took longer than Alyson had anticipated—she hadn't realized they had wandered so far during the day—and the sky had gone from brilliant pink to flaming orange, the horizon etched in black, before they finished their evening meal.

They sat around the campfire, talking lazily, drinking strong black coffee as the stars came out one by one to fill the vast western sky. Although she'd thought it would be impossible, Alyson had managed to relax, even though Sid sat only a few feet from her. That is, she managed to relax until she saw Lenny drooping over his hot chocolate, fighting to keep his eyes open. She didn't want her young cousin to fall asleep yet. Didn't he know that kids his age were supposed to have a constant supply of adrenaline pumping through them?

"Len . . . *Len*," Sid called. "Hit the sack, Jack. You're about to drown in your cocoa."

Alyson waited for the inevitable argument, the argument he always gave her, but it didn't happen. Lenny stood up, yawned and stretched, then muttered a sleepy "good night" before crawling into his sleeping bag.

What now? she wondered as panic struck. She didn't want to be alone with Sid. Not yet. She wasn't ready for it. She didn't want the intimacy of the dying campfire and the dark night, the intimacy of speaking in whispers to avoid disturbing Lenny.

Whom was she trying to kid? Just having Sid in the same universe was an intimacy she wasn't ready for. Men like him were outside her experience.

No, that was wrong, she decided. There were no other men like him. That was part of the problem. Something about this particular man had set off an inexplicable, irrevocable chain reaction in her. It was as though their meeting were part of a much larger plan, a small but necessary piece of an intricate production. It was a plan she couldn't even hope to understand. All she could do was hang on for dear life and see it through to the finish.

"You look like you're waiting for the Four Horsemen of the Apocalypse to come riding into camp."

"Hmm? What?" She glanced at him, then away again in a nervous gesture. "Oh, I—I was just trying to guess, you know, how long we would be here."

His lips curved in a distinctly unpleasant smile. "I was wondering how long it would take you to get fed up with the dirt and heat and portable john."

She sat up straighter. "Did I say anything about being fed up? I was thinking of supplies, mainly water. But besides that, have you forgotten you have a business to run? Surely you can't stay here indefinitely?"

"Indefinitely won't be necessary. And if we run out of supplies, we'll drive back to San León. It's not real complicated."

"Fine," she said, her voice stiff, her chin high. "You've answered my questions."

"Now answer one for me. Are you still getting Len mixed up in your head with his father?"

She gritted her teeth. Why couldn't he leave it alone? "I've already told you that I will have to resolve my feelings for Blair in my own way, in my own time. And frankly, it's none of your business."

"When it involves Len, I make it my business."

"It doesn't—"

"It does," he said sharply. "He's a person. He's not full-grown yet, but he's no less an individual for that, and he deserves his own identity. How do you think he would feel if he found out the only reason you tolerate him is because he's Blair's son?"

She detested the mocking way he said Blair's name. "I didn't say that," she ground out. "I *never* said that. Why are you doing this? Why do you keep attacking me?"

"Lady, you better thank Heaven I'm holding back," he said tightly. "If I followed my instincts, I'd be shaking you till your teeth rattle. You beat everything. Nothing I say, nothing I do, makes a dent in that fluffy pink armor of yours." He inhaled roughly. "You're out here in the grit and grime and heat of the *real* world, you've got a *real* kid to take care of, and you still look like some fairy-tale princess, floating somewhere above reality on a nice soft cloud. Nothing touches you," he said, staring at her with incredulous anger. "Do you understand, can you even begin to comprehend that you have that boy for *life*? If you keep this up, if you stand inviolate, letting life flow around you, Len's chances of making it are poor at best."

She flinched, feeling as though he had slapped her. The vituperative anger came at her from left field, catching her off guard. She wanted to throw vicious words right back at him. She wanted to wound him, hurt him in the same way she had been hurt. But she could only stare at him, her eyes wide with shock and pain.

Rising awkwardly to her feet, she walked away from the campfire into the enveloping darkness. It would be the final humiliation if she allowed him to see her cry.

She waited until she reached an outcropping of rock, moving behind it, hiding behind it, as she dropped to her knees and let the sobs shake through her.

Sid stood up restlessly and poured his coffee on the fire. Damn it, she was crying, he thought as he shoved his hands in the back pockets of his Levi's. It was just like her to pull that kind of feminine trip on him.

He kicked dirt on the fire a couple of times, swore violently under his breath, then left the dying fire behind to go and find her.

She was not more than twenty feet from camp, on her knees, her hands covering her face as she cried.

"Ah jeez, don't do that, Aly," he groaned. Dropping down beside her, he took her in his arms. "Come on, honey. Look . . . I'm sorry. Okay? I didn't mean it. I was just being a horse's butt."

She shook her head against his shoulder. "No, you were right," she whispered, her voice choked with tears. "Lenny is in big trouble, because I'm totally, completely useless. You didn't tell me anything I didn't know. I've always known it. I can't even *cook*, for heaven's sake. You and Lenny have to handle the food. If you hadn't decided to come with us, I'd still be back in Dallas trying to figure out how to get this thing under way."

What was he supposed to say to that? She was probably right, but he didn't think it would make her feel any better to hear him agree with her.

Dipping his head, he kissed her on the neck. "Everybody has their own area of expertise. Roughing it just doesn't happen to be yours."

"Nothing is."

He moved his mouth to her ear to suck gently at the soft lobe. "That's not true," he said huskily. "That stuff I said . . . remember what I told you in Del Rio? When I don't know how to handle a situation, I get mad. It's a defense mechanism, and even though I yelled at you, I was mad at myself."

He was telling her the truth. Alyson was a situation he didn't know how to handle. Every time he thought he had her figured out, she would throw him a curveball. She never reacted the way she was supposed to react. She was supposed to be a marble goddess. And marble goddesses didn't come to life. At least not for Sid Sweet.

"You're just being nice," she said as a hiccuping sob shook through her.

He gave a harsh laugh. "Sure, that's it. In the few days you've known me, that's the thing that's really impressed you, isn't it? You've been thinking all this time, 'That Sid Sweet—he's one nice guy.' "

"Sometimes you're nice, but always, you're honest." Her voice was defeated and still husky with tears. "The truth is, I'm an expert at *nothing*."

He pushed her hair aside so he could kiss the top of her spine. "Oh, yeah?" he murmured, his voice husky. "You have the most beautiful neck in the history of the world."

Shivering, she dug her fingers into his arms. "Even if that were true, it's a physical attribute. It's what I am, not what I do."

He took her chin in his hand and raised it, looking her straight in the eyes. "Kissing is something you do. And you have a kiss to start wars over."

She stared into his eyes, her breathing suddenly erratic. "I do?"

"You do." He lowered his head slowly until their lips touched.

And then it started all over again. The fire, the pain, the compelling hunger.

Everything he had told himself earlier had been a lie. He wasn't going to stay away from her. He wasn't going to play it cautious and safe. And he wasn't going back to camp without making love to her.

Sid knew he would have to give her up as soon as they left the mesa, but while it lasted, he would make the most of his time with her. He would make sure she would never forget him. He thanked his lucky stars there had been no other men in her life. That meant that as the first, he would always be a part of her. No one, no man who came after him, would ever make her forget her first time.

The deep brand that he, Sid Sweet, had left on her heart wouldn't be visible, but it would be with her for the rest of her life.

Alyson knew the minute he lowered her to the still-warm rock surface what was going to happen. This was why she had panicked when she was suddenly alone with him. She had been using Lenny as a shield. But not from Sid. From her own overwhelming emotions.

She should have been afraid. She was about to lose her virginity. She was about to take the biggest, most important step of her life thus far. Where was the fear? Where was the anxiety and doubt she had always assumed would attend this mysterious act of love?

It simply wasn't there. She had been waiting for this—wanting it, fearing it—since the first time he touched her. And she wasn't ashamed to admit her weakness, because the plain fact was that it had been no decision of hers. There had been no decision to make. From the very beginning, there had been no choice.

She reveled in the feel of his lips on her neck, catching her breath as he moved down to kiss her breasts through the soft fabric of her sweatshirt. Her hands moved in his hair, pressing him closer.

"Yes," she whispered. "Yes . . . *please*."

Raising his head, he gazed into her eyes. "No 'pleases,' no 'thank-yous.' Not between us. This isn't the time for nice manners, Aly," he whispered, his voice low and intense. "Take what you want." He raked a kiss across her lips. "Take what you want, because you can bet it'll be what I want too."

"Take?" she echoed hoarsely. "Anything I want?"

"Anything you want."

He had handed her freedom. With a few words he smashed all the restraints, he had ripped off the chains of civilization, that had bound her for too long. And the freedom drove her out of her mind.

Grasping his shirt with both hands, she jerked with all her strength, tearing the buttons loose, exposing the warm rough flesh of his hard chest. She reached up and placed feverish hands on his shoulders, shoving him back until their positions were reversed and she leaned over him, her hair brushing against his face.

"I want this," she breathed in a tight whisper as she leaned down and bit the place where his neck and right shoulder came together. "And this." She moved slightly and sucked at his earlobe. "And this and this." She kissed her way across his jaw and nipped his lower lip with her teeth before thrusting her tongue deep into the warmth of his mouth.

Her heart was pounding violently when she moved away slightly, jerking up the sweatshirt to expose her naked breasts. When she brushed them across his chest, he caught his breath audibly, and a husky laugh escaped her.

She was no longer the old Alyson Wilde. She was brand new. No hang-ups, no doubts, no questions. This Alyson was built especially for him. Her body had been made solely to revel in this man's touch.

Moving her hands down his body, she slipped her fingers under the waistband of his jeans. "Most of all . . . most of all, I want this," she said as her fingers found the fastening of his jeans.

"Dear sweet heaven," he rasped out, and a heartbeat later he grasped her hips and rolled with her in his arms.

He was out of control. She recognized it immediately, and it brought pleasure so intense, it drove her right over the edge. They tore at each other's clothing in their desperate effort to get closer and even closer. Seconds later the warmth of his hard bare body against hers became the ultimate erotic sensation.

Nothing was planned. Nothing was orderly. The only rules were the ones their bodies dictated, and neither of them paused at the final step. As he pushed inside her, joining them, she threw back her head, wild animal sounds catching and melting in her throat. She dug her fingernails into his biceps and met every thrust, her body moving of its own accord, taking what she needed to assuage her fierce needs and giving as much in return.

Their lovemaking was a fire storm that swept over them, fusing them together, burning them up. Alyson heard his words, low and savagely urgent, just seconds before the fury and the beauty swept her away completely.

Eight

"Aly, wake up. Come on, wake up. Breakfast is almost ready, but Sid says we can't eat till you get up."

Turning her head slightly, she shoved handfuls of blond hair out of her eyes. "Who are you?" she mumbled.

He grinned. "Your cousin Len. Sid says if you don't get up, I have his permission to roll you off the edge of the mesa." When she groaned and rolled over, burying her face in the sleeping bag, he said, "He didn't really mean it about rolling you off the edge."

Fighting her way out of the covers, she sat up. "You don't have to sound so disappointed. What time is it?"

"I don't know, but the sun's been up for hours." He studied her face. "You don't look so hot. Are you allergic to something? Your lips look puffy, and your cheeks are red, like you been sandpapering them or something."

She closed her eyes for a brief moment, then opened them. "If I'm allergic to anything, it's to thirteen-year-olds who insist on pulling up my hair to yell in my ear." She paused. "It couldn't be as late as you said. The air is still chilly."

The sun had not in fact been up for hours. It had barely cleared the horizon, the long shadows of morning still lingering on the land. But it was bright enough to shake the remnants of sleep from her mind, to bring instant vivid memories of the night before. Her pulse quickened in reaction. An incorrigible smile curved her lips, and when she moved, she felt the change in her body. It was *wonderful*. Even the soreness was wonderful.

Even the memory of making love with Sid was better than all her old fantasies combined. Back in Dallas she had decided to start taking chances, to live life on the edge, but she had never dreamed the consequences would be so thrilling.

Okay, okay, she admitted silently. So it hadn't exactly been a bold move on her part. She had been more or less swept overboard. He had touched her, and, like a dam bursting, she had gone crazy. She had—

Dear lord, she had ripped the buttons off his shirt!

Alyson didn't know whether to laugh or hide. How on earth was she going to face him?

Crawling out of her sleeping bag, she glanced around. Sid was on his haunches beside the campfire, between her and the outcropping of rocks where she always dressed, the same out-cropping that she had hidden behind the night before. She would have to pass him to change out of her sweatsuit, her official nightwear for the trip.

Maybe he wouldn't say anything. Maybe he would do the polite thing and—

She broke off the thought abruptly. Sid had told her more than once that he was no gentleman. Doing the polite thing wasn't his style. *But kindness was,* she thought suddenly. He had demonstrated the night before how kind he could be. Maybe he would feel sorry for her this morning and pretend nothing had happened between them.

Picking up her toilet kit, she walked toward the rocks, keeping her gaze anxiously on Sid. He gave no indication that he had noticed her as he settled an iron skillet on the hot coals. Hope built in her as she drew near him and he still didn't turn. She had almost passed him when she heard the low growl.

She froze in her tracks, then seconds later swiveled her head, searching in vain for Grendel. The dog was nowhere in sight.

Sid was still squatting by the fire, his back to her. As she watched, he glanced over his shoulder, and she heard the low growl again. Then he smiled and rose to his feet. "Morning, tiger."

A weak moan escaped her, and she walked into his arms, surprising them both. "Oh, Sid . . oh, Sid."

He laughed. " 'Oh, Sid' what?"

"Oh, Sid, I'm so *embarrassed*," she groaned,

holding the front of his shirt with both hands as she buried her face against his chest. "That wasn't me last night. That really wasn't me."

"It wasn't? Quick, tell me which way she went. I definitely want to keep in touch with that lady."

"It's not funny," she said, laughing against her will. "I don't know what happened to me."

He touched her hair, smoothing it down with a rough hand. "To tell you the truth, I'm a little confused about that myself. I'm pretty sure we didn't have high tea together last night, but that's about all I'm sure of."

"It was . . . it was *incredible*," she said, the words muffled by the fabric of his shirt.

"That's got to be the understatement of the century," he said, and she could hear the laughter in his voice. "I wish you could see your ears. They're the brightest red I've ever seen."

"Are they? Are they really?" she asked, her voice distracted as she felt his hand move on her hip.

"What are y'all doing?" Lenny asked, directly behind her. "Aly, why do you have your face stuck in Sid's chest?"

Alyson sighed in resignation. It was time for her to come out of hiding. "I thought I saw a loose button," she said, reluctantly releasing Sid's shirt. "Actually, I was just giving Sid his good-morning hug. Want one?"

Lenny backed away from her. "You wouldn't really hug me," he said warily.

She glanced at Sid. "He's weakening. My fatal charm is finally beginning to work on him."

"That makes two of us."

She heard the whispered words just as she

picked up her toilet kit, and she almost ran back into his arms. What on earth had he done to her?

Later in the morning they rode out again. This time, when they stopped for lunch, Sid took great pleasure in informing her that it was time for her to learn how to handle a rifle.

"Stop snickering," she snapped at Lenny, then glanced at Sid, moistening her lips nervously. "I don't think—"

"You don't have to think," he interrupted. "Just do what I tell you. Len, take those cans I brought and set them up over there on those rocks."

When Lenny ran off, Sid turned back to her. "Forget about the gun, Aly. Put it out of your mind. Just think about how much fun the lesson is going to be."

"How can I think about the lesson and forget about guns?" she complained. "The lesson is supposed to be about guns."

"I'm talking about this lesson," he said.

Turning her around, he stood close behind her, his hips pressing into her buttocks as he reached around her and showed her how to hold the rifle.

She swallowed heavily. "There might be more to this than I thought," she said, her voice shaky.

His husky laugh was warm on her ear. "If it doesn't get dark soon," he murmured, "I will go out of my mind. I need to hold you, Aly. Do you think Len will buy an afternoon hug?"

"Ready!" Lenny called at that moment. "I got the cans set up."

"Maybe not," Sid said, not bothering to hide the regret in his voice. "Okay, Annie Oakley, let's see your stuff." When she glared at him, he laughed. "I didn't mean that, not that I don't want to see that stuff too. But not with Len watching."

To her chagrin, Alyson had the makings of a sharpshooter. As soon as she overcame her fear of the rifle, as soon as she stopped holding it as though she was waiting for it to explode in her hands, she had no trouble hitting the targets Lenny had set up.

She didn't want to be good. She still didn't care for the idea of handling a gun. But when she saw how pleased Sid was with her progress, she squelched her feelings and kept up her target practice.

During the next few days, as their relationship developed, Alyson saw a side of Sid that she wouldn't have believed existed. The frustrated anger had disappeared, and he seemed always to be smiling, even laughing. He surprised her by constantly reciting poetry to her. Not the sentimental kind, of course. She recognized Poe and Kipling, but most of it was unfamiliar. He liked poetry with rhythm and punch. He told her that most junk dealers and pawnbrokers were collectors. His collection—sayings and poetry, and even tabloid headlines—just happened to be a little different. He saved anything that struck him as ridiculous, ironic, or poignant. She loved that about him. Which wasn't surprising because she loved everything about him.

The knowledge that she was in love with Sid hadn't struck her like a bolt of thunder. It had crept up on her gently, softly stealing into her heart. She knew now that when they had made love that first night, it wasn't only her physical needs she had sought to satisfy. Her emotional needs, more critical by far, had urged her on, demanding that she become a part of the man she loved.

Being in love—deeply, passionately in love— changed her in subtle, unexpected ways. She began to relish every single waking moment. The dusty, rocky world around her seemed to sparkle when she looked at it now. She still didn't like the evil-looking lizards and grotesque bugs that Lenny delighted in springing on her, but she could at least laugh at herself when the sight of them threw her into a panic.

Nights were the best. At night, after Lenny had fallen asleep, they would move Sid's sleeping bag away from the campfire and lose themselves in each other. After an entire day of being close without being able to touch, they would be desperate. And always it was as wild and frantically wonderful as the first time.

Absorbed as she was in the newfound wonder of her love, she was taken by surprise when one day Lenny reminded her why they had come to the mesa in the first place.

Her cousin had ridden ahead of them, too restless to put up with their slow pace. She and Sid, involved in their conversation, had let their horses slow to a halt when they heard the excited shouts as Lenny rode back toward them with Grendel keeping pace, barking every time the boy shouted.

"I saw something," he called out as he reached

them. "I saw something that I remember from last time."

"You saw something?" Alyson asked, sharing his excitement. "But that's wonderful, Lenny."

"Nice going, kid," Sid said. "What is it?"

"Come on, let me show you," he said, already moving away from them. "It's a bunch of rocks that look like Goofy's head on a snowman body."

Some minutes later Alyson leaned back to study the nine-foot-tall rock formation.

"Well, what do you think?" Lenny asked, glancing from her to the mound of rocks.

She tilted her head to the side to study it. "I think it looks more like Pluto's head," she said, laughing when he cuffed her on the back of the head. "I think you done good . . . as someone less grammar-conscious might say," she added hastily. "I knew you'd find something eventually, but I didn't think you would do it this quickly."

When Lenny looked at Sid, the latter smiled. "Ditto. Okay, let's get over here in the shade of Goofy's nose and poke around in your brain."

As soon as they were settled, Lenny began to chew on a fingernail, nervously glancing at the two adults. "I don't know if I can remember anything else. I mean, the rocks are the only thing around here I recognize."

"Don't start tensing up," Sid ordered. "Just relax and try to remember what you were doing the day you saw this the first time."

"I was looking for rocks for Mercedes' collection. I remember that. It was the first day we were here."

"But not the same day you saw the Madonna?"

Lenny shook his head. "Uh-uh. That was a coupla days later."

"Did you see the formation again that day?" Alyson asked.

He closed his eyes and remained silent for a while, then shook his head. "I can't remember."

"That's all right," Sid said. "Even if you didn't see it that day, you've got your bearings now. It won't be long before you recognize something else."

After Lenny had wandered off again, Sid made no move to leave the shelter of the rocks. He sat next to Alyson, watching her. Lately he couldn't seem to take his eyes off her. He had tried to tell himself, more than once, to wise up, but it didn't work. After making love to her the first time, he had shut off all thoughts of the future, taking one minute at a time.

He still was not quite able to believe what had happened between them. He couldn't get over the way she had changed in his arms that first time, the way she had gone crazy when he touched her. Although it was the first time she had ever made love, she could have written a how-to book on the subject. It was that *right* between them. It was that right.

When he had first met Alyson he thought she was the only person he'd ever met whose last name was more inappropriate than his own— Wilde. What a laugh, he thought then. This woman couldn't be wild if her life depended on it.

He'd been dead wrong. She was wild and sweet and sexy as hell. And it blew him away.

Now, sitting beside her in the meager shade, he touched her on the shoulder, not to get her attention but simply because he needed to touch her.

She glanced up at him and smiled. "Hello there," she said softly. "I wondered when you would remember that I'm here."

" 'Remember'?" he said, his voice rueful. "You're not the forgettable type. You could hit me in the head a couple of times with a sledgehammer and not get my attention more effectively." He put his arm around her, easing her closer to him. "We should have come here in winter, when the days are short. These long ones are killing me."

She laughed, and smoothed a kiss across his jaw. "I have a feeling Lenny is getting suspicious. He's not exactly a backward child."

"Does that bother you?"

She shook her head. "No, it doesn't bother me. He thinks a lot of you. It won't be any shock to him to know that I also think a lot of you."

Sid liked the sound of that. He would have liked a confession of undying love better, but he was willing to take what he could get.

"You were right about Lenny," she said suddenly. "We've gotten closer up here, and I'm really seeing him now, seeing him as an individual." She smiled. "I like what I see. Blair would have been proud of his son."

Every muscle in Sid's body clenched inward. "How can you still say his name like that, with that sickly awe in your voice?" he asked tersely. "It's damned unhealthy. Why can't you get it through your head that he just wasn't the man you thought he was?"

She jerked her head toward him, her eyes dimming, as if the anger in his voice hurt her. After a moment she said, "It's something I have to resolve on my own, Sid. Maybe I am fighting the truth, I don't know. I can't seem to let him go."

"Don't kid yourself. You don't *want* to let him go." He stood up. "A man like me could never understand someone like Blair. Isn't that what you said? Well, you got that right. I don't understand him. And I'm damned glad of it."

"Blair made mistakes—I'm trying to come to grips with that," she said, her voice softly pleading. "But should I wipe out the memories, good memories, just because he made mistakes?"

He stared at her face, feeling—right or wrong—that her continued acceptance of Blair was a rejection of him, a rejection of what they had found together.

"Keep them," he said harshly. "Wallow in them for all I care."

Alyson watched him walk away, knowing he was angry, knowing that once again she had disappointed him. And once again there was nothing she could do about it. He wouldn't let her into that hidden place so that she could understand what it was he wanted from her.

It wasn't the first time she had felt this particular fear creep up on her. Occasionally there was a look in his eyes, a certain way he held himself, that she didn't understand. It was a bleakness, a solemnity, that shut her out. At those times an aura surrounded him, a mood that was sad and vulnerable and lonely. It made her want to take him in her arms and hold him. It made her want to protect him. But when the moods struck, when the wall came up between them, she made no effort to break through. Sid was a strong man, the strongest she had ever met, and she felt there was nothing she could give him. Acknowledging that fact was a disappointment more bitter than any other she had experienced.

Throughout the rest of the day tension built steadily between them. If Sid spoke to her at all, it was to make some cutting, hurtful remark. Unable to face his contempt, she began avoiding him, slipping away from him, even when he sought her out.

After they had eaten dinner, Sid sat on one side of the campfire; she sat on the other with Lenny between them. For half an hour the boy had been trying to teach Grendel to sit up and beg.

"Give it up, Lenny," Alyson said finally. "Look at him. That animal is not going to beg, not if you offered him standing rib roast complete with frilly little paper panties. He would simply take it, along with a few of your fingers."

Lenny frowned, scratching his head. "Maybe I should teach him to roll over and play dead."

"The only way you're going to get him to look dead is to get the rifle and shoot him," she said dryly. When Grendel turned toward her and growled, she sat up straighter. "It was a joke," she said hastily. "For heaven's sake, it was only a joke."

"What have you got against Grendel?" Lenny flopped down beside her, watching the dog move around the fire to sit at Sid's side. "He's the bitchinest dog I know."

She sighed. " 'Bitchinest,' Lenny? How long did you live in California?"

"Coupla months."

"Not long enough for that word to have become a permanent part of your vocabulary. Couldn't you say 'gnarly' or 'rad'? Something with a less offensive sound to it. You could use some remedial work in—"

Lenny stood up abruptly. "Bedtime," he said, his voice innocent. "A growing body needs its rest."

"Coward," she said, laughing.

She was still smiling when she glanced across the fire and found Sid watching her, his dark eyes brooding.

She glanced away. "Bedtime," she echoed, her voice husky.

Before she could move away from the fire, he was beside her, holding her arm in a strong grip.

"Sid, please," she whispered, glancing over her shoulder to Lenny settling down to sleep. "This is not the time to discuss it."

"When is?" he demanded. "Check your calendar. I want to know right now when you're going to have time to discuss it." She avoided his eyes, and he gave a harsh laugh. "That's what I thought."

Moving her head slightly, she met his hard

gaze. "I don't see what good it would do to talk about it. You're angry with me. I can accept that. What I can't accept is why you're angry. You're mad as hell at me for being *me*. You're angry because of how Blair—"

He pulled her close, moving against her in a blatantly erotic caress. "Forget Blair. I don't want to talk about him, and I don't want to think about him. He doesn't have anything to do with this. He's just a symbol. Every time something doesn't fit into your perfect little world, you retreat from it. You simply shut it out, the way you're trying to shut me out now." He gave her a hard shake. "It ain't gonna happen, lady."

He dipped his head and kissed her. Using one large hand to grasp her buttocks, he lifted her, bringing her closer against him. "It ain't gonna happen," he repeated roughly, then abruptly released her.

As she stumbled away from him and crawled into her sleeping bag, anger began to build inside her. He was always confronting her, always forcing her to talk and think about things that made her uncomfortable.

He had destroyed their closeness with such ease. She hated him for that. He had no right to do it. He had no right to think so little of what they had together. And, damn him to hell, he had no right—so carelessly, so easily—to make her fall in love with him.

Okay, it's time I thought about it, she told herself. There was something, something in the back of her mind, that she had been hiding from. It was time to get it out in the open and face up to it.

As soon as Lenny found the Madonna, they would leave the mesa and go back to Dallas, and it would all be over. She had fallen in love with Sid, knowing all the time that she would never be anything more than an interlude. She had spent most of her life pretending, but now, when she desperately needed the comfort of an illusion, she couldn't do it. Sid had turned to her because she was there. The facts were obvious and undeniable. She was a representative of a world he despised, but because the real world was far away from their campsite, he had let her get close. For a little while. For as long as they were here. When they left, it would be over. She would be just another disposable tissue relationship.

Lying in her sleeping bag, she bit her lip to stave off the pain. Making love with him should have been the beginning of a wonderful new life for her, the beginning of maturity. That was the way it should have been. In reality, it was the end. The end of her fantasies. Sid had killed them without even knowing, even trying. By proving to her that reality was better than anything she could imagine, he had destroyed her dreams. It was a cruel, cruel thing to do. When this was over, when they left the mesa behind, she would be left with nothing. She wouldn't have him, and she wouldn't be able to escape that awful truth in dreams.

Sid stared into the fire, but he didn't see the small flickering flames. He saw her face. Everywhere he looked, he saw her face.

He hated what she was doing to him. He hated that she had so quickly become necessary to him. A society deb out looking for a little fun, a little danger, from a man who lived on the wrong side of the tracks had pulled him into her false warmth and had slammed the door behind him.

He frowned and glanced away from the fire, knowing he was being unfair. She had done nothing deliberately. She was as surprised as he was at what had happened between them. But that didn't change the facts. What they had was a temporary thing, a connection with gossamer wings and no substance. And it would dissolve into a distant memory with the first dose of civilization.

He shifted his position restlessly, wincing as he felt the pain in his leg. It had been giving him trouble lately, and he knew he should look at it, maybe apply more antibiotic ointment.

He would do it in a minute. As soon as he managed to push her out of his mind. As soon as the need for her stopped twisting him up inside.

Alyson couldn't sleep. How could she relax when she was acutely aware that Sid was not more than ten feet away? The ache, that now-familiar ache, had begun in her breasts and between her thighs, but before long it spread. Now every inch of her body throbbed with desire. Her hunger for him was eating her alive. She was shaking with it. She was dying from it.

Then suddenly he was there, scooping her up, bag and all. She gave a muffled yelp and began to struggle against him, her actions a mindless battle for survival.

"*No!*" she gasped, fighting to free her arms from the down-filled cocoon.

"Stop it," he hissed. "Do you want to wake Len?"

The question was effective. She made no more noise, but that didn't stop her from fighting him as he carried her away from the campsite. When he laid her down, a dozen yards from camp, on another sleeping bag, one that had obviously had been placed there in advance, her struggles grew more intense. She had a crazy idea she was fighting for her principles.

Unzipping the bag with one hard jerk, he freed her arms only to pin them above her head. "I'm not going to rape you," he said in a low voice. "But you already know that, don't you? It's not even me you're fighting. You're fighting yourself."

"I hate you," she whispered tightly.

"No, you don't. You tried to, the same way I tried to hate you, but neither of us managed to pull it off."

He paused, staring down at her, his features harsh, his dark eyes strangely vulnerable. "This thing between us shouldn't have happened. All the odds were against it. Hell, the odds were against us even meeting. But we did meet. And we came out here to the back of nowhere, and we made love. It doesn't matter that if we hadn't come here, it would never have happened. What matters is, it did happen. We made love, and it was good. *It was good*," he repeated, his voice rough.

"And it's going to happen again, Aly." Tears had overflowed her eyes, trailing across her temples to dampen her blond hair. He lowered his head to kiss them away. "It's going to happen right now. Are you going to keep fighting?"

She parted her lips to tell him she would fight forever, to tell him that in the most cutting, hurtful way she could find, but it didn't work out that way.

"No," she said, the word a breathless whisper. "I'm not that stupid."

She pulled her arms free of his loose grip and clasped his face with both hands to pull him down to her, parting her lips eagerly to receive his kiss.

"That's right," he said against her mouth. "Eat me up, Aly. Eat me up. Then neither of us will have to go hungry tonight."

She was still crying when he entered her. She cried in happiness and relief. She cried for the impossible beauty of it. And she cried because it wouldn't last forever.

Long after Alyson had fallen into exhausted sleep, Sid lay awake, holding her in his arms, memorizing the way she looked, studying the blond hair that had turned platinum in the moonlight. Reaching up, he ran a finger over the delicate lines of her face. At that moment he felt he could spend the rest of his life watching her. She was so damned beautiful. So loving, so giving.

He shifted his position, trying to ease the

throbbing pain in his leg. That the pain had disappeared while he made love to her didn't surprise him in the least. He had known his need for her would overcome anything.

How in hell was he going to spend the rest of his life without her? His muscles clenched suddenly. Dammit, he didn't want to give her up. And at the moment he didn't know which would be worse—not having her or knowing that some other man would. The thought of another man touching her was like a wound in his gut, but he knew it would happen. She was too alive, too damned sexy, to stay alone for long.

It was ironic, almost laughable, that when Sid finally fell in love, it was with the one woman he could never have. Someone like Aly wasn't for the likes of Sid Sweet.

Alyson came awake slowly, and it took awhile for her to realize Sid was muttering incomprehensible words in her ear.

A nightmare? she wondered.

To soothe him, she reached up to stroke his face, then sucked in a sharp breath. He was burning up with fever.

"Sid," she said, shaking his shoulder. "Sid, wake up. You've got a fever."

He didn't respond to her touch or her voice. He kept muttering and shifting his body restlessly. It was when she pushed free of the sleeping bag to stand up that she heard a noise and turned her head swiftly toward it.

It was Grendel. The dog was crouching next to Sid on the other side, and he was whimpering.

If Alyson had been scared before, she was now petrified. With uncanny perception, Grendel knew something was terribly, terribly wrong.

Scrambling to her feet, she pulled on her discarded sweatsuit and ran to camp. When she returned, she carried a canteen and a washcloth, stumbling in the darkness in her rush to get back to him.

Grendel growled low in his throat when she approached. He was guarding Sid and didn't want her to get close to him. Without a second thought, she merely pushed the snarling dog out of the way. Kneeling beside Sid, she began bathing his face in the cool water.

Please God, she prayed in urgent silence, *please don't let anything happen to Sid. I couldn't bear it.*

"What is it? Why are y'all out here? What's wrong with Sid?"

She jerked her head up when she heard Lenny's frightened words. Although she hadn't heard him approach, he was not two feet away, his thin arms wrapped around Grendel's neck, and he looked as scared as she felt.

"He has a fever." She couldn't keep her voice from shaking. "I don't know what's wrong with him, Lenny. I'm just trying to bring his temperature down." She pushed her hair back with trembling fingers. "It's all I could think of to do."

Lenny's eyes were wide in the moonlight. "Do you think it's his leg?"

She frowned. "His leg? What's wrong with Sid's leg?"

"Didn't you notice? He's been limping for a couple of days. I asked him about it, but he said it was nothing."

She didn't speak for a moment, then she said, "Get the lantern, Lenny."

He was back in seconds. Together they pulled down the top layer of the sleeping bag. When they reached his thighs, Alyson's heart jerked in her chest.

It must have been the barbed wire. On his left thigh was a long gash, swollen and purplish-red in the lamplight, and angry-looking streaks radiated from it.

"Sweet heaven," she breathed in a horrified whisper.

"Is he going to die?"

She swung around on her heels toward Lenny. She wanted to grab him and shake him silly. Then she saw the terror in his eyes.

"No, of course not." She put her arm around him and pulled him close. "Of course Sid's not going to die."

"Daddy did," he said, his voice hoarse and uneven. "Maybe it's that curse thing Father Mike was talking about. Maybe God doesn't want me to take the gold statue back. Maybe it's not supposed to go back until a angel comes to get it." He met her eyes. "If we told God right now that we'll leave, do you think he'll let Sid get well?"

"Oh, honey," she murmured, brushing the tangled hair from his face. "There's no curse. God isn't doing this. Sid ran into a piece of rusty barbed wire, and he obviously didn't take care of the cut. God didn't make him act stupidly." She forced a smile. "He did that all by himself. So we don't need to make any deals for Sid's life."

"But what are we going to do?"

"We're going to take care of him," she said firmly. "You and I are going to take care of him. And whatever it takes, we'll make sure he gets well."

Nine

Sid was delirious throughout most of the night, and several times it took both Alyson and Lenny to hold him down. Seeing this strong man—a man they had both come to think of as invincible—brought down by illness left them both panic-stricken. But only for the first few hours. After that weariness numbed them, and they simply did what they had to do. They had neither the time nor the energy to spare for thoughts of what had been in the past or what might be in the future.

Although Sid's fever didn't break, it dropped considerably when the night began to dissolve into day. As the world around them gradually lightened, Lenny lay on top of his sleeping bag—he had moved it during the night near Sid's—and stared at the horizon, as though silently urging the sun to keep its promise and rise over the horizon.

Abruptly, he rolled over and looked at her. "Tell me again how you and me, we're going to take care of everything."

The look in his eyes was unmistakable. It said last night had left him shaken. It said he had no confidence in himself and even less in her. Alyson didn't blame him. She was scared, too, but she had to hide it. If she ever let the fear out, she would fall apart completely.

Lenny depends on me to be strong, she thought, swallowing something that was a cross between a helpless sob and a hysterical giggle.

"We don't know nothing," he continued. "Sid's the one who knows. He's the one who takes care of things."

She held a damp cloth to her burning eyes for a moment, then said, "The French have a saying. 'In the land of the blind, one-eyed men are king.' "

"Huh?"

"It means we're all we've got. The two of us are it," she said, smiling to hide the tremble in her lower lip. "Sid can't take care of this, and there's no one else. So by the process of elimination, we're elected."

He took a moment to digest this. "So what do we do now?" he asked finally.

"We discuss our options. I was waiting for daylight to get him down to the Jeep, so we could take him to the hospital. But I'm afraid I didn't even stop to think about what getting him off the mesa would involve," she admitted ruefully. "It would seem that Sid took care of the thinking as well as everything else."

She drew in a deep breath. "The thing is,

Lenny, I don't know if we can get him on his horse. If by some miracle we managed to lift him, we would have to tie him on. Then one of us would have to lead the horse every step of the way to make sure it didn't stumble and go off the edge."

Her words conjured up a too-vivid picture. They stared at each other for a long moment. Then Lenny swallowed and said, "What are our other choices?"

"I could go down alone. That would mean leaving you here while I drive back to San León to bring a doctor to him." She moistened her dry lips. "A round trip would take most of the day, and I'm not sure I could get back before dark. It's just not possible to come up the trail at night, so you would probably have to spend the night here alone with Sid."

Lenny glanced away from her, concealing whatever fears might be showing in his eyes. "What else?" he asked roughly.

She pushed back her tangled hair. "Our third option is to treat the wound ourselves. We would have to lance it and—" she broke off and cleared her throat, "we could apply hot compresses to draw out the infection."

Did he know she was faking it? Alyson wondered. Did Lenny guess that she had no idea what she was talking about? She had never treated a wound. She had never even cared for a sick animal, much less a man.

"What if we made something like a stretcher? You know, those things the Indians pulled behind their horses. That way we wouldn't have to lift him."

"That's a good idea," she said, genuinely impressed. "But what about those rocks? Do you think maybe the trail would be too rough?"

His thin shoulders slumped in defeat. "They would beat him to death," he said tonelessly. "Which one do you vote for? I'll stay with him if you want me to. I don't mind. Really. Grendel will be with me, and . . . well, I could take care of Sid okay, by myself."

"I know you could, honey. You would take care of him just fine. But I don't think that's the best way to handle it. I think it would be better if we start caring for his leg right now instead of waiting a whole day for a doctor to get here and do it."

Lenny stared at her for a moment, then let out a deep breath and sat up straighter. Until that moment she hadn't known how much he had been dreading staying there alone.

"I vote for that too," he said, his voice stronger. "What do you want me to to?"

She moistened her cracked lips. "You could heat some water. We need clean hot water. Two pots of it. Do we have two pots, Lenny?"

It seemed to Alyson that every passing second brought some reminder of how incompetent she was. She didn't even know what utensils they had in camp.

But there was no help for it, she decided, straightening her back. "And we'll need to boil one of my cotton shirts. A white one. I can use it to make compresses."

When Lenny jumped up to leave, she called him back. Avoiding his eyes, she said, "I— Lenny, I forgot about the knife. It will have to be sterilized too. Would you find a sharp knife—"

"A knife?" His voice was high and scared again. "Why do you need a knife?"

"To lance—" She broke off, realizing Lenny didn't know what the word meant. Exhaling slowly, she met his eyes. "Honey, I'm going to have to cut him. I have to cut open the wound so it can drain."

Lenny turned white, and for a moment she was afraid he would pass out. "Do you . . . are you sure?"

She wasn't sure of anything. Not one damn thing. But she didn't know what else to do. Heaven help her, she didn't know what else to do.

"It's the only way," she whispered hoarsely. "If it gets worse, he might lose his leg— I shouldn't have said that. I'm sorry, Lenny. Please don't worry about it. If it ever reaches that point, we'll get him off the mesa, even if we have to carry him off ourselves."

Strangely, hearing there was a possibility that Sid might lose his leg seemed to strengthen Lenny. His thin features tightened, and he stood up straighter. "I'll go find a knife," he said without further comment.

The next two hours were a nightmare straight out of hell. Each separate event, every small move Alyson made, became crucial in her own mind. The boiled water had to cool to precisely the right temperature. Each knife had to be tested to see which was the sharpest. The knife and strips of cloth had to be boiled for exactly ten minutes. She became preoccupied by minutiae.

When she actually held the knife in her hand, when it finally struck her that she was really going to do this, Alyson almost threw up. Only Lenny's presence beside her kept her from breaking down completely. Only the thought of the man she loved kept her hand steady.

Then suddenly it was over. She had done it. She had lanced the wound, drained it, and begun the application of hot compresses.

Sid hadn't stirred once through the entire process, and at the time she had been grateful. Now it began to worry her. She kept telling herself that he had worn himself out during the night. He was simply too exhausted to feel what she was doing to him. She wasn't sure if she believed that or not, but she allowed herself only a few seconds of shivering and shaking fear, then kept going.

In all the time she had known him, even when she'd loved him most, Alyson had never thought of Lenny as a blessing. But throughout the day he proved to be exactly that. He performed every task she gave him, readily and without complaint. Of his own accord, he took care of the horses. And he took care of her. He made sure she ate, and he even brought her soap and water and a brush, so she could feel more human.

Later, much later, she sat on her sleeping bag and stared out at the distant view. Lenny had built a fire several feet away from the sleeping bags and was now taking a turn at watching Sid. Alyson hadn't wanted to leave him, she never wanted to leave him, but she knew she would have to rest to take care of him during the night.

Now, staring out at the horizon, she shivered.

She had known it would happen. It happened every day, without fail. But as she stared at the sinking sun, a cold hand gripped her heart. She wasn't ready for night to come. Illness was always worse at night. People died at night.

Surprisingly, Alyson drifted off. She hadn't expected to sleep, but when she opened her eyes again, it was dark. In the firelight she saw Lenny, sitting beside Sid with his arms wrapped around his knees. He looked exhausted.

She rose to her feet. "You get some sleep now," she whispered as she approached him. "You were an angel to take over for me. I feel one hundred percent better."

He didn't argue. He could only nod sleepily and crawl into his sleeping bag. Within minutes he was asleep.

It was less than an hour after Lenny had fallen asleep when Sid's fever began to rise again and the delirium returned. Instead of a constant restless mumble, tonight he talked in starts and stops.

At first she could make no sense of his rambling speech, but gradually the words became clearer and stronger. As she bathed his body with cool water, Alyson was given glimpses of Sid's past. She heard about his childhood with his grandfather, the isolation that came with being poor and parentless. With no clear pattern he jumped from the triumphs to the fears to the unimportant. At one point, while in the grip of past anger, he hit her across the chest with his forearm, knocking her on her back. She didn't even cry out. She simply scrambled up and threw herself on top of him, holding him down until the rage passed, concerned only that he do no damage to himself.

The worst was when he talked about women, women he had known and been involved with. Eventually, inevitably, he seemed to concentrate on one particular woman. Someone he had loved. Someone beautiful and sexy. Someone who had hurt him.

Alyson hated the woman, but she was also contemptuous of her. The anonymous woman from his past had held heaven in her hands, and she had thrown it away because she didn't think Sid was good enough for her.

She dipped the cloth in water, wrung it out, and applied it to his forehead. "Forget her," she told him firmly.

It didn't matter that he couldn't hear her. Last night and again tonight she had talked constantly to him. In some way talking to him kept her going.

"Whoever this 'Miss Manners' is, she's not worth even a minute of your time," she continued. "If she was too stupid to see what a wonderful, loving man you are, worth a dozen ordinary men, that's her problem. She doesn't deserve you."

In her one-sided conversations she told him many things, but most often she told him of her love. It was the only chance she would have to say it aloud, and she couldn't say it often enough. She told him how he had changed her life, how he had kissed her and shaken her awake. She told him how empty her life had been before he came along and how empty it would be when he left her.

She was telling him how she had felt in his office on the day they met when he began to shake. Without warning, violent shudders racked through his weakened body.

"Oh, dear God, no," she whispered.

Throwing aside the damp cloth, she crawled into the sleeping bag with him, pulling him close, trying to surround him with her warmth.

"Aly?" His voice was hoarse and almost inaudible. "Lord, I had the weirdest dream. Making love on your fluffy pink cloud. Just disappeared. Dissolved. Arms full of nothing." He shivered. "Crazy to be scared of a cloud. You're here. Didn't dissolve."

"I'm here," she whispered, cradling his head on her breast as she stroked his hair. "I'll always be here, darling. Didn't you know that?"

The moment of lucidity was gone, even before she finished speaking. He had drifted away from her again. Throughout the night she held him in her arms, and with silent, urgent prayers she willed him to get better. She willed her strength into his body.

Sid heard the voices before he came fully awake. It was major work to open his eyes, so he gave up the struggle and kept them closed. He could see vivid colors against the backdrop of his closed eyelids and figured it must be daytime. And judging by the heat, the day was pretty well along.

He couldn't believe he had slept so long. It must have been that scratch on his leg. He had intended to put more antibiotic ointment on it, but he'd been distracted by the way Alyson was avoiding him, and he had forgotten.

You stupid fool, he condemned silently. He had Lenny and Aly to take care of. He had responsibilities. He couldn't afford to let his damned leg get infected.

He would get up in a minute and let them know he was back on the job. In a minute, he thought just before he fell asleep again.

The next time he came awake, he managed to open his eyes enough to see that the sun was almost directly overhead. Alyson and Lenny were standing several feet from him.

Frowning, Sid studied them. Something was wrong. Something had changed. Lenny wasn't slumping, or biting his nails, or ducking his head when she talked to him. And Alyson . . .

When Sid turned his gaze on her, he blinked rapidly. She looked like warmed-over death. Her beautiful blond hair fell in thick tangles around her face, and there were dark circles under her eyes. Her skin was tight and unnaturally pale, and if he hadn't known it was impossible, he would say she had lost weight overnight.

She pushed at her hair, trying to tuck it behind one ear as she talked to Lenny. "Do the horses seem restless to you?" she asked. "Should we turn them loose to get some exercise?"

"I'll take care of the horses in a minute. But first I'm gonna watch Sid while you get some rest."

She raised one haughty brow. "Are you giving me orders, little boy?"

"You got it," he said firmly. "What are you going to do about it?"

"I was just asking," she said meekly, and they both laughed.

They not only looked different; they sounded different. Confidence blazed out of Lenny. It was in his voice, in the way he held himself. And she—she looked at ease, comfortable in her surroundings. She looked as though she belonged there.

Twisting her shoulders, she rubbed her lower back. And as she turned toward her sleeping bag, her eyes met Sid's, and she saw him watching her. Instantly her gray eyes grew cloudy with worry.

Sid's lips twisted in a slightly mocking smile. "You lose your comb?" he asked, his voice hoarse and raspy.

Alyson stared, wide-eyed for a moment, then closed her eyes and swayed on her feet.

"Len!" Sid yelled, fighting to get out of the sleeping bag so he could go to her.

Lenny ran back to Alyson and threw an arm around her waist to keep her upright. When he held her secure, he shot a glance toward Sid. "She's just a little tired," the boy explained, his voice apologetic. "How do you feel?"

Sid frowned. "How should I feel? I'm hungry."

Unaccountably, Alyson covered her face with both hands, and her shoulders began to shake with harsh dry sobs.

Lenny laughed and pulled her closer in a hug.

"Hey, stupid, he's okay now." He shook her. "You hear me? He's okay."

Dropping her hands, she stared at Sid and whispered, "He's okay. Lenny, *he's okay!*"

Lenny laughed again then moved back to slap her hand in a high five. "*Now* will you get some rest?"

She nodded without taking her eyes off Sid. "But first," she said, "there's something I have to do."

"Will you two tell me what the hell is going on?" Sid demanded irritably.

Alyson walked to where he lay and knelt beside him. Framing his face between her open hands, she kissed him, long and hard and passionate.

Sid struggled to get his arms free of the sleeping bag so he could hold her, but before he could manage it, she broke off the kiss.

A moment later she drew back and hit him in the shoulder. "Don't you ever, ever make fun of my incompetence again!" she yelled. "Even a *brainless idiot* knows to take care of an infected cut!"

With that she stood up, staggered to her sleeping bag, and crawled inside. She heaved a long sigh, and in the next instant she was asleep.

After a moment Sid turned to look at Lenny. "You want to tell me about it? I take it I've been sick."

Lenny laughed. "Sick? You were almost dead."

Sid raised one heavy brow in skepticism. "Aren't you exaggerating a little?"

"Maybe, but not much," Lenny said, then proceeded to tell him about the events of the past three days.

"See, at first she tried to fake me out and pretend like everything was fine," Lenny said. "She was pretending like she knew what she was doing. But one night I woke up, and she was crying. I think she was too tired to pretend. She said it was all a fake and she was scared to death because she didn't know what she was doing. I know this sounds weird, but I felt better after that, knowing she was as scared as I was. And like she said, being scared doesn't make any difference. There was stuff that had to be done, scared or not."

Sid clenched his fists. If anyone else had done this to her, he would have tried to kill him, but how did he give himself the beating he knew he damn well deserved? Then, as Lenny continued to talk, telling him everything that had happened, Sid realized he was taking his beating—a bloody no-holds-barred beating—without anyone raising a hand to him.

When Lenny paused, Sid glanced at him, puzzled by the flush that had spread across the boy's face. "What is it, Len? Did something happen you're not telling me about?"

Lenny nodded. "But it's not about you. It's about me. Last night you were kinda resting easy, so we were just sitting there talking, and— I don't even remember what started it, but all of a sudden we were talking about Daddy."

Sid glanced away from the boy's eyes. "She thought a lot of your father," he said stiffly.

"She loved him," Lenny said. "Just like me. It

was weird, Sid. I didn't even know I was mad at Daddy until Aly told me she was."

"She said she was mad at Blair?"

He nodded. "Real mad. She said she still loves him, she'll never stop loving him, but she was mad because he didn't protect me. She said it was his job and he didn't do it." Lenny shook his head. "I always thought I would slug anybody that talked bad about my dad, but . . . see, she loved him like I did. That made me see that it was all right for me to be mad at him. It's all right if I think he wasn't so perfect."

"He was a good man," Sid said slowly. "But he was human, and he made some mistakes. Bad mistakes."

"That's what Aly said. And she said Daddy would want me to do better than he did. He wouldn't want me to make the same mistakes he did."

Sid smiled. "It sounds like you and Aly did a lot of talking."

"We didn't have much else to do." He paused. "You know, Sid, Aly counted on me. I mean, she really needed me to help her. She said she couldn't have done it without me."

Lenny's pride was unmistakable. It was in his voice, shining from his eyes.

"I'm proud of you too, son," Sid said softly. "It looks like you saved my butt for me."

Lenny shook his head. "Not me. It was her. I did what I could to help, but she's the one who did it. She wouldn't leave you for anything. I think she would have cut off her arm if it would have made you get better."

Sid glanced beyond Lenny to where she lay sleeping. "Why do you suppose she did it, Len?" he asked in genuine confusion. "I mean, why did she do more than she had to, more than was strictly necessary to help me?"

Lenny shrugged. "That's just the kind of person she is. She would have done the same for anybody."

Moving slowly, Sid lay back on the sleeping bag and closed his eyes. It was a while before he spoke again. "Yeah," he said, his voice weary. "I guess you're right."

Ten

Sid walked slowly to the edge of the mesa, using the cane Lenny had made for him, and stared out across the rough wild country.

It wouldn't be long before they would be ready to leave. It was almost over. Now, now that the end was almost upon him, Sid almost regretted that he had ignored the looks Alyson had been throwing his way for the past two days.

He shifted his position restlessly. She wanted him. She wanted him almost as much as he wanted her. But Sid had to ignore her desire, using his leg as an excuse. He couldn't let himself do anything about those looks.

He had decided years ago that sex without emotion wasn't for him. The decision had been an objective one, one that barely disrupted his life and certainly caused him no grief. But this time he was in love. The decision not to make love to her was eating away at him, gnawing at his insides. But he couldn't give in to the need. Making love to her, knowing she didn't love him, would destroy him.

She cared about him. She might even feel a certain degree of fondness for him. But it just wasn't enough. He wanted—he *needed*—her to love him as much as he loved her.

Fat, freakin' chance, he told himself with mocking self-derision. Someone like Alyson wasn't for the likes of Sid Sweet.

Exhaling a rough breath, he turned and made his way back to camp. When they got back to San León, he would let a doctor look at his leg. They would probably spend the night in Lenny's hometown before driving to Del Rio the next day. Then they would say good-bye.

Lenny didn't seem disappointed that they hadn't found the Madonna. He said he wanted to come back some day, he wanted to keep looking for it, but the urgency was gone. Lenny had found himself without any outside help.

Before he made it all the way back to camp, he saw Lenny riding hard toward them. Although the boy was still quite a distance away, Sid heard his whoops over the sound of the horse's hooves on the rock surface.

Alyson joined him just as Lenny reached them. He pulled back on the horse's reins, making it rear slightly, then jumped down and began a wild pagan dance around the two adults, accompanied by Grendel's frenzied barking.

"Lenny!" Alyson shouted. "For heaven's sake, calm down. What are you doing?"

He grabbed her by the waist and waltzed her around. "I'm dancing. Come on, Aly, let's boogie," he said, laughing.

Stopping abruptly, he looked at Alyson, then at Sid. "I found it. Well, really, Grendel found it, but he didn't know what it was, so I really found it."

"The Madonna," Alyson said, her eyes wide.

Grinning, Lenny nodded. "I found her."

Alyson sat on the cool dirt that covered the floor of the cave, her gaze trained on the small golden statue.

"Isn't anyone going to pick her up?" she asked quietly.

She glanced at Lenny, then at Sid, but neither of them moved toward the lost Madonna.

It had taken them over an hour to clear away enough rock to gain entry to the small cave. Fallen rock took up most of the space, but Alyson had a feeling the cave had once been much larger. Only the area around the tiny niche that held the Madonna had remained free of debris.

Lenny moved to sit beside her. "I know we gotta take her back, but—"

She put an arm around his thin shoulders. "I know how you feel. She looks natural here, doesn't she? She looks like she belongs."

They both jumped when Sid kicked at a pile of fallen rock. "That's stupid," he said harshly. "You know how much the gold in that statue is worth? And even if she were made of plaster of paris, she wouldn't belong here. Hell, she doesn't even belong in that little dirt-poor church." He glanced back at the Madonna, then at Alyson. "She's class. And class always gravitates toward its own kind. She belongs somewhere that's as classy as she is, with people as classy as she is."

Alyson was silent for a moment. "Don't you think— I mean, isn't it possible that she would rather be in a place where she's genuinely loved, where she's genuinely needed, than be surrounded by a lot of impersonal 'class'?"

Lenny looked from one adult to the other. "Are y'all talking about leaving her here? You wouldn't really do that?"

Sid moved to the niche and gently picked up the Madonna. "No, we wouldn't do that. She goes back to Saint Lucy's. I was just talking to hear my teeth rattle."

Alyson knew better. She didn't know what was behind the anger he had shown moments earlier, but she knew it was real and deep. And it was just one more thing about him that she didn't— would probably never—understand about him.

Holding the statue with gentle care, Sid turned to Lenny. "Here you go, kid. She's yours to take care of until we get back to San León. Think you can handle it?"

Lenny wiped his hands on his jeans and glanced nervously at Alyson. When she smiled and nodded, he reached out and took the Madonna. "Sure," he said. "I can handle it just fine."

Alyson lay on the bed in San León's only motel. She wore a cotton-knit undershirt that fit snugly across her breasts, ending at her midriff, and matching bikini panties.

Sid's room wasn't next door as it had been in Del Rio. It was all the way across the courtyard, as far away from her as he could get.

Lenny had chosen to spend the night with his friend Jacob. So far, only a few people in town knew what had happened, that the Madonna had come home, but enough knew to make Lenny look about six inches taller.

Alyson had met Mercedes. The little girl Lenny used to play with had grown into a young beauty. At first Lenny treated her exactly as he treated Jacob. As though the years hadn't passed. As though they were all still best buddies. At some point it hit him that not only was Mercedes gorgeous, but she had a giant crush on him. That was when his attitude had changed. Seeing Lenny flirt was odd to say the least.

Rolling over on her stomach, she punched the pillow a couple of times, reshaping it to fit her head. Although the motel room was small and plain, it was clean, and the bed was soft. It should have been a welcome change, but for all the notice she took, she could still be lying on the hard rock on top of the mesa.

She wished very much that she were sleeping on the rock again. She would gladly have spent the rest of her life on the mesa. As long as she had Lenny and Sid with her. Sid had to be there, or it would just be a desolate spot in the middle of the badlands. Sid had to be there, or the grandest, most elegant house in the world would be a desolate spot in the middle of the badlands.

Sid had changed, even before they reached San León. As soon as they mounted their horses to begin the long climb down, she noticed the difference. He didn't treat her with contempt as he had when they first met, and he didn't challenge her as he had continually during their time on the mesa. His attitude was casual and congenial. Polite and friendly. He had found the perfect way to put a wall between them.

Glancing around the room, she saw the pink sweatsuit she had laid carefully on a chair. If she had any sense, she would burn it as soon as she got home. But of course she had no sense where Sid was concerned. So instead of burning it, she would put it in her bottom bureau drawer and save it. When she was an old lady, she would pull it out and remember how her one and only love had taught her about the pleasures of her body. And about love in general.

Moaning, she told herself not to think about it. She couldn't allow herself to think about it. But neither could she lie there feeling sorry for herself. Those times were past.

Moving abruptly, she pulled herself up to sit on the side of the bed. She couldn't pinpoint the moment it had happened. She wasn't even sure there was a single cause, but however and whenever it had happened, she had changed up there on the mesa. She was stronger now. Strong enough to go to him and risk being humiliated by his rejection.

If it had to end, she would have one last time.

Before she lost her nerve, Alyson picked up the telephone and punched in his room number.

"Sid," she gasped as soon as he answered, "Sid, there's something— You've got to help me! Hurry, Sid. *I need you!*"

She dropped the receiver and stared at it with a mixture of horror and chagrin. She had really done it now.

Only seconds later she heard his anxious knock on the door. When she opened it, he rushed in, his left leg still stiff.

"What is it?" he said urgently as she closed the door behind him. "What's wrong?"

She met his eyes. "I told you," she said calmly. "I need you."

His gaze dropped, took in the way she was dressed, then glanced away. "Cute trick, Aly," he said, his voice carefully casual.

She swallowed in nervous reaction. "The thing is, I'm not strong enough to pick you up and carry you away, the way you did that night. That's not very fair. You wanted me, so you just picked me up and took me. Well, I want you now, so I had to get you here in my own way."

He didn't respond, and although the silence made her even more nervous, she refused to back down. She had gone too far.

"The times we've made love," she said quietly, "it's been a pretty desperate kind of thing. You felt that, didn't you? I mean, you felt that we were more or less carried away by the situation, and we both went a little wild. The thing is, Sid, just once before this is over, I'd like to make love *on purpose*. I want it to be a deliberate thing, something we've thought about and decided would be a

. . . well, a good thing to do. Can you understand that?"

For a long time he simply stood there and stared at her. Then he turned and opened the door.

"No!" Moving quickly, she grabbed the room key out of his hand and pushed it down her top, between her breasts. Raising her chin, she said, "Now you can't go back to your room."

He shook his head, one brow raised, his lips twitching with laughter. "Wow," he said slowly, "that'll sure stop me." Then he reached in and pulled out the key.

"Goodnight, Aly," he said as he walked out the door.

The rocks and dead plants in the courtyard hurt her feet, but she was close behind him when he reached his room, close enough to have the door slammed in her face.

"Go to bed, Aly," he said through the door.

She glanced over her shoulder, searching for her room. The light that should have been shining out the open door was missing. Probably because the door wasn't exactly open. She must have closed it without thinking when she ran after him.

"Sid," she said softly. "Sid, my door is closed, and I left the key in my room."

"They have extras at the front desk."

"But I'm in my underwear. Oh, no . . . Sid, someone's coming," she hissed in an urgent whisper. "Just let me in for a minute. Please, Sid. I could wear one of your—"

The door swung open, and he moved aside to

let her pass. "Why are you doing this?" he asked in exasperation. "It ain't etiquette. You're breaking all the rules of polite society. That's not like you, Aly."

"Yes, it is. At least, it is now. See, I grew. Up there on the mesa I expanded my range of possibilities." She glanced at him, biting her lip. "I just wanted to be with you again. Is that a crime? If you didn't want me chasing you, you shouldn't have started it in the first place. You should never have shown me what it's like."

He walked two paces away, pushed a hand through his hair, then looked back at her over his shoulder. "I want you to go back to your room, Aly," he said.

She was getting to him. His voice was no longer casual. His fists were clenched, and he held his shoulders stiffly.

She held his gaze for a moment, then shook her head in two short jerky movements. "Noooo," she said softly. "I don't think so."

He turned his head away from her, and in the long silence that followed, she stared at his back, her arms wrapped around her waist. "Don't you want me anymore, Sid?"

He sucked in a harsh breath, and when he turned, his brown eyes were blazing. He moved the two steps that separated them and grabbed her by the waist, jerking her against him. One hand came up behind her head as he kissed her. It was wild. Savage. Out of control.

"*No*," she gasped, pulling away.

"What the hell do you mean, 'no'? Isn't this what you came here for?"

Her hands shook as she placed them on either side of his face, smoothing her thumbs across the taut flesh covering his cheekbones. "Please, Sid," she whispered, staring into his eyes. "I love it wild. And it would be so easy to let the wildness sweep me away again, but . . . but just once, let me see the tenderness. I need the sweetness tonight, Sid."

He closed his eyes tightly. "How can I touch you without going wild?" He rasped out the words. "It's not circumstances that made me lose control. It was you. I get near you, and I go crazy." Opening his eyes, he gave a harsh laugh. "It's not exactly something I turn on and off."

She stared up at him, her lip trembling. "I just—" she broke off and shook her head weakly, "I only . . ."

When he lowered his head to kiss her, it was as soft and gentle and sweet as she had wished. "I can't keep it from turning wild, Aly," he said. "But maybe we can do a deal. We can have it sweet"—he ran his tongue across her lips in a subtly erotic caress—"and wild." He shoved both his hands inside her panties to grasp her buttocks, jerking her closer, fitting her against him. "Sweet and wild," he said again. "Deal?"

A helpless moan escaped her, and she dug her fingernails into his shoulders. "Deal. Sweet"—she kissed his throat—"and wild," she echoed, sinking her teeth into the same spot.

And that was the way it was. He smoothed sweet tender kisses on the bruises he had inflicted during his illness. Then he added some new ones with the fierceness of his wild desire.

She had wanted Sid to make love to her one last time, knowing it wouldn't be enough, believing it was all she would have.

But she was wrong. When the first rays of the sun came through the window, he still held her in his arms as he made love to her again. One last time.

The churchyard was full. All seven hundred and five citizens of San León were crowded onto the grounds of St. Lucy's, along with half a dozen dogs and, incredibly, a goat. They had all come to see the Madonna and the boy who had brought her home.

Lenny was a hero. The men slapped him on the back, the women hugged and kissed him, and his peers crowded close to bask in the glow of his glory. Alyson wouldn't have been surprised to see Lenny hoisted up on the shoulders of the good people of San León.

He would almost certainly come out of it with a swelled head, but she didn't mind. It would all even out in the end. A little idolizing would be a welcome change for him.

All morning Alyson had watched Sid mingling with the people. He was in his element here, laughing and swapping stories.

He was a special man, she decided, this man who was hers.

The possessiveness she felt toward him surprised her. What surprised her even more was the fact that she liked the feeling. Of course, to be strictly honest, he didn't exactly know yet that he belonged to her. But he would. She would make sure of that. She would wear him down, no matter how long it took. When they returned to Dallas, she would haunt the pawnshop. She would use Lenny, with no compunction at all, to get closer to Sid. She would dog his steps until he broke down and let her into his life.

Her gaze drifted to where he stood across the yard from her, and she stared at him until finally, as though he felt her eyes on him, he turned his head toward her.

She sent him a slow smile. *Prepare yourself*, she told him silently. *I've just declared war.*

The sun was dipping low in the sky when the crowd at the church finally began to clear. The last few people trickled out of the church, the same look of awe and wonder on each face, as she joined Sid and Father Mike.

"I suppose I'd better get on down to the party at the community center," Father Mike said with a smile. "One of my less popular duties is to make sure they don't celebrate enough to wake up with hangovers tomorrow." He glanced at Sid. "I like what you've been saying, Sid. Could you come by my office tomorrow to expand on some of those ideas?"

Sid nodded, then leaned against the church wall, watching the priest climb into a battered station wagon.

"You know, Sid," she said, leaning next to him, "I've been thinking about Lenny. He's got a really good relationship with you. I mean, it isn't hero worship like it was with his father. It's a more solid thing. And, well, I think it's good for him.

If you don't mind, I'd like for him to spend more time with you in the future. Maybe you could come out to the house on weekends, and—"

"I'm not going back to Dallas," he said abruptly, interrupting her carefully prepared speech.

She felt an iron fist grip her chest, and she straightened away from the wall, staring at his face with stunned eyes. "What do you mean? What are you talking about?"

"I've decided to stay here." He smiled. "You're not the only one whose range of possibilities has been expanding. I told you I wanted to join the Peace Corps. Well, I think I can do what I want right here in Texas, right here in San León." He paused. "They need me here. They need a fast-talking hustler, someone to help them hold on to the Madonna. And Father Mike is thinking about cooperative farming. That means they'll need someone to cut through government red tape for them. Someone who can give the establishment types a good swift kick in the butt." He met her eyes. "That's me."

Fighting against panic, her mind began to work furiously. She moistened her lips. "Yes . . . yes, I see what you mean, Sid. Did I ever tell you about my contacts in government? Through my family, I've met quite a few of them, state and national. And several in agriculture," she added, trying to keep desperation out of her voice.

He didn't look at her. "It would help if I could use your name." He smiled. "A little clout never hurt anything."

"Actually, I was thinking of something a little different," she said. "I . . . I might stay and help."

She gave a nervous laugh. "Committees are my specialty. I know how to play the games, and I'm really very good at organization."

Finally, he looked at her, his eyes narrowed, his lips white. "Why? Why on earth would you want to stay here?"

She shrugged. "Why not? Even before we came here, I was getting tired of my life in Dallas. I was tired of doing distant good deeds. I need more of a hands-on thing." When he simply kept staring at her, she shoved her hands into her skirt pockets. "Of course, I won't stay if you'd rather I didn't."

Moving away from the wall, he took a couple of steps away, his back to her.

"Okay," she said in frustration. "Okay, I'm a coward. We both know that. But I'm going to be as honest as you always are. It will hurt like hell, but I guess it's time." She drew in a deep breath. "Are you ready for a good laugh? I want to stay here because I can't stand the thought of leaving you. I would stay anywhere to be near you."

When the silence drew out, she felt pain wash through her in waves. "Say something, damn it. Do you want to see the rich princess get down on her knees and beg? Is that it? Well, I'll do it," she whispered. "If it will do any good, I'll beg, Sid. Just . . . just say you'll let me stay."

"Playing with fire, Aly?" He didn't look at her as he uttered the stiff words. "Do you need to let a little crudity into your life to break the monotony?"

She had no idea what he was talking about, but she recognized the contemptuous tone. "At least look at me," she said, her voice shaking. "Have the decency to look at me when you insult me. Is it too much to ask that you look me in the eye when you throw my love back in my face? I may not be much in your estimation, but you can at least—"

He swung around abruptly, and the look was on his face again. The sad, lonely, vulnerable look. "What did you say?" he rasped out.

"I . . . I said look at me." She exhaled a tremulous breath. "I just wanted—"

"Not that." He reached out, his movements awkward, as he touched her face. So gentle. So sweetly gentle. "You love me?" he whispered.

She clasped a hand to her mouth, holding back the tears and desperate laughter. "Please, don't. Don't you dare pretend you didn't know. Sweet heaven, I've done everything but tattoo it on my thighs. I chased you shamelessly. I even tried to be what you wanted me to be, trekking through the wilderness, shooting that damned rifle. I did everything I knew how to do, Sid," she said, her voice breaking. "And it didn't work. You still shut me out."

With a swift urgent movement, he pulled her into his arms, holding her so tight, he took her breath away as he pressed his face to her neck. And suddenly the words were pouring out of him.

"You wanted me to be tender, and I couldn't tell you . . . you didn't know that I couldn't be gentle. I was afraid if we ever touched with tenderness, I would break down and cry." He gave a harsh laugh. "I was afraid I would make a fool of myself and cry all over you. I'm just . . . I'm just so damned in love with you. I didn't want to ever let you out of my arms. I knew I would have to, I knew that as soon as we left the mesa, I would have to let you go, but I kept seeing these damned visions. I could see you, big with my baby in your belly. I saw myself beside you, holding your hand when our little girl was born. A little girl! Judas priest, Aly, I even knew what she would look like. And I could see me and Len taking her to the park, and when people said, 'What a pretty little girl,' I would smile and tell them she looked just like her mama." He exhaled a long, shaky breath. "I saw us turning into a couple of flaky old people, embarrassing our grown kids by kissing in public. And— Aly, I saw you there, holding my hand when it was my time to go."

He shuddered against her. "It just got so *big*, Aly. It kept growing, and I couldn't stop it. It grew until I knew . . . and this part was bad, really bad. I knew that if I couldn't have all that with you, I wouldn't have it with anyone. It wouldn't make sense with anybody else. I could see me spending the rest of my life with nothing but those damned visions. Those lousy fantasies."

She was shaking as hard as he was when she began to spread urgent kisses across his hard face. "The fantasies are gone. Do you hear me? They're gone. For both of us. Do you really think you're going to get rid of me? It ain't gonna happen, darling. It just ain't gonna happen."

It took another half hour for the frantic emotional high to subside in them, allowing them to be close simply because that was where they wanted to be. And it was when the urgency eased that she glanced up and saw Lenny.

He stood alone near the church entrance. The hero was gone, and a lonely excluded boy had taken his place.

Following her gaze, Sid smiled. "You got a minute, Len?" he yelled without letting her out of his arms.

Lenny moved slowly toward them, looking at neither directly. "Yeah?" he mumbled when he reached them.

"We need your help, kid," Sid said. "See, we were about to discuss our plans for the future, and I figured you ought to have a say in what happens. The way I see it, you've got two choices. We could track down your mother and take steps to make sure she takes care of you."

"We could get counseling for her, Lenny," Alyson said. "We can hire someone, a housekeeper or maid, to make sure she doesn't fall into her old bad habits."

Lenny still didn't look at them. "What's the other choice?" he said after a moment.

Sid held Alyson's gaze. "We're in the process of getting a family together. It's kind of bare bones right now though. What we need is a smartmouth kid to flesh it out some. It would be Aly, you, me, and Grendel. What do you say?"

"You want me?" He glanced at them, then quickly glanced away again. "You both want me to stay with you? To be your kid?"

When Sid nodded, Alyson said, "We both want you."

"I love Mom," Lenny said, the words stiff and halting. "And she loves me."

"Of course she does."

"But that's not enough, is it?" Finally he raised his head to look at them. "Just loving someone isn't enough. I don't think Mom's grown up enough to have a kid."

"Then maybe you'd like to stay with us?" Alyson asked gently. "We need you, Lenny. Do you think you could put up with us for the rest of your life?"

He turned away abruptly and wiped his eyes on his sleeve. After a moment he turned back to them and shrugged. "Whatever," he said, then grinned and ducked when his new parents broke out in laughter and both tried to cuff him on the back of the head.

Sid threw one arm around Lenny's shoulder and the other around Aly's waist, and together, the new family walked into the church.

In an alcove near the chancel, the "Golden Madonna" was bathed in the glow of rose and amber lights. On the floor below her, a large brown dog was resting, looking strangely at peace, as though his joyless journey had finally ended.

THE EDITOR'S CORNER

There's something a little bit forbidden about this month's group of heroes. For one reason or another they seem to be exactly the wrong men for our heroines to fall in love with—but, of course, the six ladies involved do just that, unable as they are to resist the potent allure of these special LOVESWEPT men. And what they feared was forbidden fruit turns out to be necessary to their very existences!

In **TROPICAL HEAT,** LOVESWEPT #432, Patt Bucheister creates a noble hero named John Canada, and she puts his nobility to the test by having him fight his overwhelming passion for Salem Shepherd, the woman he'd first known as a young girl. Together they had escaped from an orphanage and forged a friendship based on trust and need. But the feelings that began to surface in John as Salem blossomed into womanhood scared him, tempted him, thrilled him—and made him realize he had to send her away. Years later Salem returns to help John when his business is in trouble, and the feelings he'd once felt for her pale in comparison to the desire he knows he can no longer fight. These two people who've shared so much find themselves swept away on a current stronger than an ocean surge, right into the arms of destiny. Patt has outdone herself in crafting a love story of immense emotional impact.

Charlotte Hughes gives her heroine something of a dilemma in **RESTLESS NIGHTS,** LOVESWEPT #433. How can Kelly Garrett get on with her life as an independent single mom, when she discovers she's falling for Macon Bridges, a man who represents so much of what she's struggled to put behind her after her first marriage failed. Macon is the successful owner of the firm she works for; he has the tendency to want to take control and do things for her that she's just learned to do for herself; he's dedicated to his job and at times allows it to take top priority in his life. Then again, the man can charm the birds from the trees and certainly knows how to send Kelly's heart into flight! But

(continued)

once this smitten lady makes up her mind to risk it all on the sexy man who's causing her too many restless nights, it's Macon who doesn't stand a chance! Charlotte's lighthearted style makes this story pure entertainment.

TEMPESTUOUS, LOVESWEPT #434, by Tami Hoag, not only describes the feisty heroine in the book, Alexandra Gianni, but also the state of the atmosphere whenever she encounters hero Christian Atherton. The sparks do fly between the aristocratic charmer who is used to having women fall at his feet not throw him to the ground, and the lovely wildcat with the haunted eyes and determined ways of a woman who has something to hide. At first Christian sees winning Alex as a challenge, until he becomes thoroughly enchanted by the spirited woman he yearns to know all about. His wicked reputation seems in jeopardy as he longs only to soothe Alex's sorrow and shower her with tenderness. But not until Alex convinces herself she deserves to be cherished can she accept Christian's gift of love. This poignant romance features several characters from two of Tami's previous books, **RUMOR HAS IT,** #304, and **MAN OF HER DREAMS,** #331, the most notable character of which is hero Christian, whose love story you've asked Tami for in your letters. Enjoy!

Joan Elliott Pickart's **TO LOVE AND TO CHERISH,** LOVESWEPT #435, opens with a dramatic scene that won't fail to grip you. Imagine meeting a stranger in the foggy cocoon of night on a deserted beach. In a moment of yearning desperation, imagine yourself surrendering to him body and soul, then running off without ever learning his name! Heroine Alida Hunter was lost in her grief until she met the man with the summer-sky eyes. But she knew he was a fantasy, a magical gift she could never keep. Paul-Anthony Payton couldn't forget the mysterious woman who'd bewitched him then vanished, and he vowed to find her. She'd filled him with hope that night on the beach, but when he finally does find her, his hopes are dashed by her denial of what they'd shared.

(continued)

Alida's fear of loving and losing terrifies her and prevents her from believing in Paul-Anthony's promises. But the more she tells herself he's the forbidden lover of her dreams, the more Paul-Anthony makes her dreams become reality. Once again Joan delivers a powerful love story LOVESWEPT fans will treasure.

Judy Gill casts another memorable character in the role of hero in **MOONLIGHT MAN,** LOVESWEPT #436. Judy orchestrates perfectly this romance between Sharon Leslie, a gifted musician in whose heart the music has all but died, and Marc Duval, a man who's endured an unbearable tragedy and learned to find beauty and peace in the music he plays. Marc sees how Sharon is drawn to and yet tormented by the melodies he sends to her on the wind—as she is to his mesmerizing kisses. He knows she doubts herself as a woman even as he awakens her to pleasure beyond anything she's ever known. But until he can earn Sharon's trust, he can't know why she keeps turning away from him—and once she does trust him, he realizes he will have to confess the black secret of his own past. Caught up in the rebirth of the music inside her, Sharon revels in her feelings for Marc, but it all comes crashing down on her when she discovers the truth about the man she now loves with all her heart. Judy gives us a shining example of how true love conquers all in this wonderfully touching romance.

Fayrene Preston continues her SwanSea Place series with **JEOPARDY,** LOVESWEPT #437. Judging by the hero's name alone, Amarillo Smith, you can expect this to be one sultry, exciting, dangerous romance that only Fayrene can write—and you won't be disappointed. Heroine Angelica DiFrenza is surprised and intrigued when private investigator Amarillo, her brother's partner, asks her to dinner—the broodingly handsome detective had always seemed to avoid her deliberately. But when they finally end up alone together, the passion flares hotter than a blast furnace, and they both realize there's no going back. Amarillo couldn't deny

(continued)

what he'd felt for so long, but the time wasn't right. He was desperate to protect Angelica from the danger that threatened her life, and he needed a clear head and un-involved emotions to do it. But Amarillo's tantalizing kisses create a fever in Angelica's blood and the maelstrom of uncivilized hunger they'd suspected brewed between them rages out of control. You'll want to follow these two along on their journey of discovery, which, of course, leads them to beautiful SwanSea Place.

We promised you more information about our LOVESWEPT hotline, and here it is! If you'd like to reach your favorite LOVESWEPT authors by phone, all you have to do is dial 1-900-896-2505 between October 1 and December 31 to hear exciting mes-sages and up-to-the-minute information. You *may* call and get the author in person! Not only will you be able to get the latest news and gossip, but just by calling and leaving your name you will be entered into our Romantic Getaway Sweepstakes, where you'll have a chance to win a grand prize of a free week for two to Paris! Each call you make will cost you 95¢ per min-ute, and winners of the contest will be chosen at random from the names gathered. More detailed in-struction and rules will appear in the backs of our November, December, and January LOVESWEPTs. But the number will be operational beginning on October 1 and ending on December 31!

Get your dialing fingers ready!

Sincerely,

Susann Brailey

Susann Brailey
Editor
LOVESWEPT
Bantam Books
666 Fifth Avenue
New York, NY 10103

FOREVER
LOVESWEPT

SPECIAL KEEPSAKE
EDITION OFFER
$12⁹⁵
VALUE

Here's your chance to receive a special hardcover Loveswept "Keepsake Edition" to keep close to your heart forever. Collect hearts (shown on next page) found in the back of Loveswepts #426-#449 (on sale from September 1990 through December 1990). Once you have collected a total of 15 hearts, fill out the coupon and selection form on the next page (no photocopies or hand drawn facsimiles will be accepted) and mail to: Loveswept Keepsake, P.O. Box 9014, Bohemia, NY 11716.

FOREVER LOVESWEPT
SPECIAL KEEPSAKE EDITION OFFER
SELECTION FORM

Choose from these special Loveswepts by your
favorite authors. Please write a 1 next to your first
choice, a 2 next to your second choice. Loveswept
will honor your preference as inventory allows.

Loveswept®

_____BAD FOR EACH OTHER   Billie Green

_____NOTORIOUS   Iris Johansen

_____WILD CHILD   Suzanne Forster

_____A WHOLE NEW LIGHT   Sandra Brown

_____HOT TOUCH   Deborah Smith

_____ONCE UPON A TIME...GOLDEN
        THREADS   Kay Hooper

Attached are 15 hearts and the selection form which
indicates my choices for my special hardcover Loveswept
"Keepsake Edition." Please mail my book to:

NAME:_____

ADDRESS:_____

CITY/STATE:_____ZIP:_____

Offer open only to residents of the United States, Puerto Rico and
Canada. Void where prohibited, taxed, or restricted. Allow 6 - 8
weeks after receipt of coupons for delivery. Offer expires
January 15, 1991. You will receive your first choice as inventory
allows; if that book is no longer available, you'll receive your
second choice, etc.

THE SHAMROCK TRINITY

☐ **21975 RAFE, THE MAVERICK**
by Kay Hooper $2.95

☐ **21976 YORK, THE RENEGADE**
by Iris Johansen $2.95

☐ **21977 BURKE, THE KINGPIN**
by Fayrene Preston $2.95